A TALL DARK STRANGER

Joan Smith

A TALL DARK STRANGER

WHEELER
PUBLISHING, INC.
ROCKLAND, MA

★ AN AMERICAN COMPANY ★

Published in Large Print by arrangement with
Ballantine Books, a division of Random House, Inc.
in the United States and Canada.

Wheeler Large Print Book Series.

Set in 16 pt. Plantin.

Library of Congress Cataloging-in-Publication Data

Smith, Joan, 1953–
    A tall dark stranger / Joan Smith.
        p.   cm.—(Wheeler large print book series)
    ISBN 1-56895-347-X (hardcover)
    1. Large type books.   I. Title.   II. Series.
[PR6069.M4944T35   1996]
823'.914—dc20   96-20472
                                                                CIP

Chapter One

It was beautiful in the water meadow that morning. May had just arrived, but already the warm air held a foretaste of summer. Reflections of the cloud-strewn sky shone on the calm water as clearly as images in a mirror. I could even see a pair of swallows magically swooping about on the water's surface. And greenery everywhere, with the air soft as mist against the skin.

It was the greenery that had brought me to this isolated spot. My goal that morning was to sketch a fritillary I had spotted the day before. You might know the plant by the name checkered daffodil. Hereabouts it's less elegantly called snake's head. Before the petals open, it does resemble a snake's head, or it would if there was such a thing as a purple snake. The petals are a light purple, with a pattern like a snake's skin, or a fish's scales, in darker purple.

I opened my watercolor box, an elegant mahogany affair trimmed in brass, given to me by my Aunt Talbot on my last birthday when she finally accepted that I was serious about my art. The box is my pride and joy. It is every bit as handsome as a fine lady's tea caddy. It has a handle like a reticule, drawers for vials and brushes, and compartments for dry blocks of watercolor paint.

I settled on a table rock at the edge of the water meadow and opened my sketch pad. The fritillary was an easy sketch. The flower was simple, the stalk narrow with two long, linear leaves, one just below the flower, one an inch or two lower. I sketched the flower in pencil and then painted in the proper shades of purple. The fine detailing of retracing the pencil lines with black China ink would be done at home. If it turned out well, it would be varnished and added to the growing collection of paintings that would eventually be bound as a book and placed in the library at Oakbay Hall.

My chosen subject is wildflowers. Aunt Talbot and apparently Lollie feel it would be more lady-like to sketch tame ones. We have a very nice terraced garden at Oakbay Hall with roses, daffodils, delphiniums, etc., but it is their poor cousins, the wildflowers, that attract me. One can see in them the parent of the gaudy, unnatural blooms the gardeners have forced into existence. A cultivated garden makes me think of the Marriage Mart in London, where simple country girls are teased and scolded and refined into dashing flirts.

My younger brother, Lawrence—we call him Lollie—was with me that morning. He doesn't share my passion for wildflowers. His notion of pleasure is in killing innocent wild creatures, preferably with a gun. This morning he was fishing. The stream that periodically floods the meadow is a clean chalk stream deep enough to hold trout. I hadn't seen any fish in the meadow, but an occasional splash told me there were either fish or frogs present.

Aunt Talbot and I are trying to convince him to go to a university, but he will have none of it.

"What help will Greek and Latin be in running Oakbay Hall?" is his unanswerable question.

None, but it would give him the air of a gentleman. He inherited the family estate two years ago. Papa's steward, Mr. Jenkins, runs the place, but in justice to Lollie I must own he is rapidly mastering his chosen trade.

He even looks like a farmer, with his ruddy cheeks and smattering of freckles. He is a good, strong lad whose only deficiency is a lack of elegance in his appearance and manner. His chestnut hair is straight and tends to poke out at odd angles. His brown eyes are bright and his smile ready. He will settle down and make a fine landowner in another year or two.

He had been fishing around a bend in the meadow, where a growth of willows cut off my view of him. I heard his approach and began putting away my equipment. We had been there an hour, which is about as long as his patience lasts. I could stay all day, but it is considered unsafe for me to wander our own estate unescorted. The most dangerous animal afoot is a fox. Rabbits are more plentiful.

"I say, Amy, are you about ready to go home?" he asked.

3

"In a moment," I replied, rinsing out my brushes in the water. They would be properly cleaned the minute I reached home.

"Who's the fellow with Maitland? Did you get a look at him?" Lollie asked, peering across the meadow.

"I didn't notice anyone."

"You don't mean Morris Maitland crossed your path and you didn't notice! By the living jingo, you're more keen on drawing those weeds than I thought."

You may be wondering at Lollie's hint that Morris Maitland means something to me. I confess he does, but alas! I mean no more to Morris Maitland than the fritillary means to Lollie. I glanced across the water meadow for a glimpse of my idol. There was no mistaking him. He is built like a Greek god. His golden curls were covered by his hat, but there isn't another pair of shoulders like his in the parish.

"I don't recognize the fellow with him," Lollie said.

As we watched, Maitland and another man turned about and headed off toward Maitland's meadow. Our lands touch; the water meadow is the boundary between them. Maitland's estate is much grander than Oakbay Hall. Other than Lord Hadley, Maitland is the most important gentleman in the parish. None can touch him for appearance. I didn't recognize the man with him, either. Maitland spends much of his time in

London and has frequent visitors. Usually ladies make up part of his house parties.

"They're going into the shepherd's hut. That's deuced odd!" Lollie said.

Lollie has, as have I, the countryman's curiosity about our neighbors. The men were both on foot, which seemed odd. A walking tour of the estate was not Maitland's customary manner of entertaining his guests. If they had been mounted on a pair of prime bloods, it would have seemed more natural.

I looked across the water and noticed Maitland was looking around in a way that I can only call guilty—as if he was checking to make sure he wasn't watched. If it was not for the man with him, I would have suspected he was meeting a female. He has a bit of a reputation that way. He didn't look in our direction. He just stood aside and touched his friend's shoulder, ushering him into the hut.

"He's up to something," Lollie said.

"I can't see what mischief he can be up to in a shepherd's hut and with another man."

"Well, arranging something, then," Lollie said. "A cockfight, I wager. Or a gambling session. They say Maitland gambles like a fool."

"He must be lucky at cards. His estate certainly isn't suffering."

"Nor is he," Lollie admitted. "Did you see that spanking-new mare he was riding in Chilton Abbas on Saturday?"

I hadn't seen it. I had been too busy ogling Maitland, but I had heard plenty about the mare.

"Let's stay here until they leave. I'm going to scoot over to the hut," Lollie said. "They might invite me to the cockfight."

I was delighted at the reprieve. I opened my sketch pad and began drawing a monkeyflower that grew at the water's edge. Folks were beginning to introduce this modest yellow flower into their gardens. No doubt it would be forced into some unnatural growth once the professional gardeners got their hands on it. The buds were just forming. I sketched the plant in this state. I would return later when it was in fuller bud, then in bloom, and then again when the seed pods were forming. I make up a composition of the plant in various stages of growth and arrange them artistically on the same page, each phase dated.

After Lollie wandered off, I became so engrossed that I even forgot Morris Maitland. When I looked up from my work, I saw Lollie coming toward me with his fishpole over his shoulder and two small trout dangling from it. They'd make no meal for humans, but the cats would enjoy them. Lollie was accompanied by the stranger. Of Maitland there was no sign.

"This is Mr. Stoddart, Amy," Lollie said, and introduced me to the gentleman.

Stoddart was a slender fellow, very gentlemanly in his speech and manners but undistinguished physically. He had sandy hair, blue eyes, and a weak chin.

"You're a friend of Mr. Maitland's, I think?" I asked, offering him my hand. When I achieved my twenty-second year, I dispensed with curtsying.

"Not really," Stoddart replied. "I was just out walking and met him. We shared a cheroot while he waited for his friend to join him. I fear I was trespassing, but he was very nice about it. He's a decent chap, I expect. Well, *you* would know."

He seemed to be waiting for an answer. We assured him that Maitland wasn't the sort to bring out his gun only because someone was on his land as long as that person wasn't poaching.

"He gave me directions to the graveyard," Stoddart said.

Lollie had already extracted the story and gave it to me briefly.

"Mr. Stoddart is on a walking tour for his health," he said. "He believes he has, or had, some relatives hereabouts. He's staying at the Boar's Head in Chilton Abbas. He couldn't get a line on his relatives, but he thinks they might be buried here."

"What is the name?" I asked Stoddart.

Oddly, he hesitated a moment before answering. Something in his expression struck me as out of kilter, not quite honest. He wore a rather cunning expression, but he finally did come up with a name. "Fanshawe," he said.

7

"Rupert and Marion Fanshawe. They were living here in the last century."

"So was I, but I never heard of them," Lollie said. "There are no Fanshawes hereabouts."

"They might have died before you were born," Stoddart said. "It was my grandmother who mentioned them."

He looked around, then asked if we minded if he sat and rested a while before going to the graveyard.

"I'll just finish up my sketch," I said, and went to work on the complicated leaves again. Stoddart watched a moment, offered a few compliments, then began to chat to Lollie. Their talk was inconsequential. I heard Lollie pointing out the boundaries of Oakbay Hall and Beauvert, a neighboring estate, then the intricacies of sketching completely occupied my mind.

When I had finished my work, they were deep in a discussion of some boxing match that was to occur the following week ten miles away. Stoddart didn't think he would be around in a week's time. With nothing better to do, I began to sketch him.

The human face is not really my forte, but I turn my hand to it for family and friends. How else will posterity know what we looked like? You notice much more about a person's appearance when you try to sketch or paint him or her. I noticed, for instance, that Stoddart's head was longer than most people's. His eyes were just a trifle uneven; one was a small fraction of an inch higher than the other. His cravat was intricately arranged, his jacket exceptionally well cut.

I suddenly heard Lollie say, "We'll go with you." I looked up in alarm to see what he was getting "us" into.

"We pass within yards of the graveyard," Lollie said to me, "so it will be no trouble to show Mr. Stoddart where the new graves are situated."

I like graveyards. Aunt Talbot calls me ghoulish, but it's the wildflowers I like and the peace and serenity, not the touch of death. I would stop and gather some wildflowers to put on my parents' graves and on the grave of the sister I never really knew. Beth Anne died at three months. I have only the vaguest recollection of being allowed to hold her in my arms. If she had lived, she would be seventeen now, a year younger than Lollie. It would have been nice to have another young lady at Oakbay Hall.

Stoddart insisted on carrying my paint box. He told us a little about himself as we went. He was from Bath, where his papa was a clergyman.

"At Bath Abbey?" I asked, impressed.

Again that look of cunning was in his eyes. "No, not the abbey," he said. "The cathedral."

"But Bath Abbey *is* the cathedral," I said in confusion. I had not the privilege of much travel, but I had been to Bath with my parents some years before.

"Oh, Bath Abbey, of course. I thought you meant the other abbey, the Cistercian one, is it? Yes, at Bath Abbey, the cathedral. A beautiful building, isn't it? I do love those old Norman cathedrals."

I knew by this time that Stoddart was shamming it. Bath Abbey is famous for its Gothic architecture. I said nothing but went on to catch him out in a few other errors. He praised the riding, for instance, when all the world complains of Bath's hilly terrain. His toilette was too stylish for a clergyman's son as well.

We reached the graveyard. It is behind St. Peter's Norman church, tucked into a wedge of land facing the road between Oakbay Hall and Maitland's place. While I gathered my bouquets, Stoddart looked about for any graves marked Fanshawe, but there were none. If his relatives had been buried here, their graves would be in the northwest part of the yard, near my parents' graves. The older ones were to the south.

"The only Fanshawe hereabouts is Mr. Murray's wife," I said, "and she is very much alive. She was a Fanshawe before marriage, but she is not from this parish. I believe she came from London." Stoddart expressed no interest in her.

"Murray is our M.P.," Lollie mentioned.

It was getting on toward lunchtime. Sensing some dishonesty in Stoddart, I did not invite him home to lunch. Perhaps if I had, things would have turned out differently. But that is hindsight. We pointed out the route back to Chilton Abbas to Stoddart and then went home.

"He seems a nice fellow," Lollie said. He is as

friendly as a pup. As long as a man doesn't actually insult him, he is ready to call him a friend.

"He is a liar, Lollie," I said, and told him my reasons.

"By Jove, I thought Maitland had a sneaky look about him as they went sliding into the shepherd's hut. I thought he was probably meeting a woman, but when I got there, they were just having a cheroot. I shall go back this afternoon and see if I can find out what they were up to."

"Talking leaves no trace," I told him, very much in Aunt Talbot's know-it-all way. I must watch that sad tendency. Omniscience is well enough at nine and forty, but not at two and twenty. We continued on home.

We went in at the back door as it is impossible to go to the water meadow without picking up a few traces of mud.

"You'd best make it quick. She's waiting for her lunch," Cook warned us.

She, Aunt Talbot, didn't like waiting for her lunch. We darted upstairs to tidy up, thinking no more about Stoddart. We had no notion of the importance he would assume in our quiet lives. No notion that murder and treachery swirled around this stranger. All I knew was that he wasn't from Bath, as he claimed.

11

Chapter Two

If Methodists ordained ladies, Aunt Talbot would make a good clergyman. She has a fine disapproving air of anything that smacks of entertainment. In appearance, she is tall and thin. Her auburn hair, her best feature, is bound in a tight knob and covered with a cap. Yet despite her sour expression and plain dressing, she has a natural air of elegance, which I envy.

I have a similar shade of hair and I wear mine short and loose. Auntie's elegance is entirely lacking in me. I stand five feet five inches and have a well-rounded figure. Not fat, just rounded! My fingers are usually smeared with paint or ink, my gowns splattered with mud or powdered with dust. Lollie tells me my best hope of nabbing a *parti* is my eyes and my dot of fifteen thousand pounds. My eyes are green and adequately lashed. Mama left me her dot, as Lollie was to inherit Oakbay Hall.

Aunt Talbot is our paternal aunt, Papa's spinster sister. She arrived in our lives three years ago when Mama died. We were already beyond redemption. I, at nineteen, was not about to be bear-led by a poor relation. On the contrary, we are slowly but surely leading Maude Talbot into a life of dissipation.

She now accepts a half glass of wine with dinner; none for lunch. It gives her the megrims if taken when the sun is up. She accompanies us to the local assemblies, strictly in the line of duty. She goes to the card parlor but won't touch cards. She gossips instead or tells the ladies' fortunes.

You may well stare to hear such a stickler for propriety reads palms, but so it is. The little touch of Beelzebub that lingers in the best of us must find some outlet. Auntie does not just read palms; she reads the whole hand. Auntie (and Lollie, too) has an earth hand: short palm and short fingers. These characteristics denote a hard-working, no-nonsense personality. I am afflicted with a water hand: long palm and long fingers, denoting one who lives with his or her head in the clouds and is impractical—in short, artistic.

I got my water hands clean more quickly than Lollie despite my unreliability, however, and went below to distract Aunt Talbot from a lecture with a recital about the stranger met in the meadow. She is a glutton for gossip of any sort. When life offers no great doings, the small ones such as a passing stranger assume a large interest.

"The man—I refuse to call a liar a gentleman—is no better than he should be," she declared. "A man who lies about his past has some evil to conceal. But then who can you expect to meet if you go trolloping about the countryside looking like a commoner? When God gives a lady no children, the devil sends nieces and nephews in their stead."

That "looking like a commoner" was a dig at my oldest sprigged muslin. I have two or three such gowns that really ought to be dust rags, but they are too useful for my fieldwork.

"Hardly the countryside, Auntie," I objected. "I was in our own meadow. And Mr. Stoddart didn't do anything."

"I don't call lying nothing. A man who will tell an untruth will do worse. And posing as a clergyman's son! I'm surprised Mr. Maitland didn't run him off. But then Maitland is a perfect gentleman. Almost too good. He never suspects a trick."

Auntie entertains the forlorn hope that I will nab Maitland. Either that or she is so smitten by his beauty that she fails to hear the gossip about him. Age seems no innoculation against Maitland's charm.

Lollie joined us and we were finally allowed to listen to Auntie say grace and then eat. Afterward, since the day was too fine to spend a minute inside, I took my sketch pad and watercolor box to the orchard and sketched a yellow loosestrife that grew between the trees. When I tried of that, I dipped into my well-thumbed copy of Gilbert White's *Natural History and Antiquities of Selborne* to read about nature.

Lollie didn't get to the shepherd's hut to investigate, after all. A friend invited him to course hares and of course he was off like a shot to kill more harmless animals.

We had company for dinner, which made it

impossible for me to finish work on the morning's sketches. This didn't bother me. There were the long winter evenings to do the finely detailed work. Spring and summer were spent on the sketching outdoors.

The next morning I was back at the water meadow by nine. Lollie accompanied me to pacify Auntie, but in fact he intended to scoot off to oversee the sheep shearing.

"You'll be safe as churches for an hour or two, eh, sis?" he asked before leaving.

"Yes, I'm fine." I began looking about for a subject to sketch. "What is that blue thing amongst the bulrushes? Not a flower, surely? There are no water lilies here."

I peered at the flecks of blue through the bulrushes that swayed in the middle of the water meadow. The water swells in the spring and the bulrushes ring the edge of the water for the rest of the year.

Lollie got a branch and began poking at the blue thing. "Looks like Maitland's people are using the water for dumping trash," he called. We share the water meadow with Maitland. Half of it is on his property. "It's an old jacket. I'll have a word with Maitland."

He tried to hook the edge of the branch under the material, but the branch bent. Looking at Lollie, I saw his jaw fall open. He came to rigid attention, like a pointer on the scent of game.

"There's someone in the jacket," he said in a high, disbelieving voice.

I dropped my precious watercolor box and darted to join him. I saw a head bobbing in the water, facedown. The branch wasn't strong enough to pull the body to the edge of the water. In his excitement Lollie waded in and dragged the body out by its topboots. Once on dry land he turned the body over. I was overcome by an unusual fit of maidenly reluctance and turned my head aside.

"Good God, it's Mr. Stoddart!" he exclaimed.

That was enough to make me turn around. It was Stoddart, all right. He hadn't been in the water long enough to become discolored or bloated, but he was entirely waterlogged. He was certainly dead. His open eyes stared at the heavens; his mouth was slack. He looked pathetic with his face as pale as a fish's belly and his sodden hair plastered against his forehead, but he was recognizable. There were no visible marks of violence on him.

I looked at Lollie in consternation and noticed that his face was as pale as the corpse's.

"He must have drowned," I said, returning my gaze to the body and musing on the uncertainty of life.

"What should we do?"

"One of us should go for help. The other will stay here with the body."

"It's odd that he'd drown in ten inches of water," Lollie said, and bent over the body to examine it. "He must have fallen and knocked himself unconscious. Odd there's no bump.

Good lord!" he exclaimed. "Take a look at this, Amy!"

"What is it?" I asked. I didn't want to "take a look" at whatever it was, but I glanced down to see what Lollie was doing. He had opened the jacket.

"He's been stabbed!" he exclaimed. "I noticed the hole in his jacket. It goes right through the shirt. The water's washed the blood away, but he was stabbed right enough."

I didn't look at the evidence. After a momentary surge of nausea, I said in a hollow voice, "Then you'd best send for the constable."

"You'll stay with the body? Wouldn't you rather I stay?"

"Yes, much rather."

I turned to leave, then turned back. "Come with me, Lollie. No one can harm a corpse, but whoever killed him might be lurking nearby."

"Stoddart's been dead for hours. His killer wouldn't stay around. I'll be all right, but hurry."

He needn't have suggested it. I flew through the meadow as if pursued by a madman, trampling wildflowers underfoot in my dart, which is something I would not usually do. The rank grass entwined my ankles, as if to hold me back. The trip had never seemed so long. Finally, I ran, gasping, into the house and fell onto a chair in Cook's steamy kitchen. I was grateful for the comfort of the familiar servants, the stove and aromas of cooking.

"Dead," I gasped.

Cook turned as pale as paper and grabbed the edge of the table. "Not Master Lollie!" Cook hasn't yet adjusted to calling Lollie Mr. Talbot, though I have become Miss Talbot.

Her helper, Inez, screamed. Betty, the scullery maid, came darting out of her lair carrying a plate and a tea towel. She dropped the plate and it broke with a clattering noise.

"Oh, no! Not Lollie," I assured them. "There's a body in the water meadow. The man's been stabbed. We must send for Monger."

Inez and Betty screamed in unison and hugged each other for comfort. "Stabbed! We'll all be kilt." That was Betty.

"A murderer! I ain't going out into the garden for vegetables," Inez averred.

"Hush up, you silly girls," Cook said. "Who'd bother to murder the likes of you?" On this piece of cold comfort she turned back to me. "Who was it, a stranger?"

"Mr. Stoddart."

"Oh, the man you and Master Lollie met yesterday." There are no secrets in a small household such as ours.

"Yes. I'll send George to Chilton Abbas to fetch Monger." George is our footman, the only male house servant other than Lentle, our aging butler. We have grooms and gardeners outdoors, but in the house George is our factotum. I don't know how we would get along without him. "I'd best tell Auntie first," I said.

"She's doing a reading. Mrs. Murray stopped by."

Mrs. Murray is our local M.P.'s lady, *née* Marie Fanshawe. Whenever her husband brings her home from London, she entertains herself by swanning through the village in overly elaborate gowns, flirting with all the local fellows and having her fortune read by Auntie. In the earlier days she had held card parties, but once the local ladies discovered the high stakes she played for, they were always busy when she called.

As soon as I had caught my breath, I ran upstairs and into the Rose Saloon. Our less worthy neighbors have their palms read in the morning parlor, but as the carpet and curtains there are well past their prime, such notables as Mrs. Murray are entertained in the Rose Saloon. It is a beautiful, lofty chamber, full of sunlight on that morning in May. Mama had redone it just before her death. Mama always liked to be in fashion.

I stopped a moment in the doorway to compose myself. Auntie was examining Mrs. Murray's hand. I knew from my own observation that Mrs. Murray was afflicted with club thumbs. It is the only flaw in an otherwise perfect physical specimen. She is a blond, blue-eyed, porcelain-skinned lady who is, incidentally, twenty years younger than her husband but still more than a decade older than myself.

According to Auntie, those clubbed thumbs indicated an unmanageable temper and a coarse, violent nature. I had seen no evidence of these character flaws. Her nature was flighty and vain; I would hardly call her either violent or coarse.

"Oh, Miss Talbot," she said, glancing up. "Have you had a spill? I see your gown is all muddied."

"There's a dead man in the water meadow," I said. "Mr. Stoddart. He's been stabbed."

"Oh, my!" She lifted both hands to her lips. The clubbed thumbs marred the beauty of ivory fingers and flashing diamond rings. "You're sure he's dead?"

"He's been dead for hours, I should think."

"The devil you say!" Aunt Talbot gasped. "Stabbed? You mean . . . murdered?"

"Yes. We found him floating amidst the bulrushes. Lollie stayed with him."

"Stoddart, you say? That's not a local name," Mrs. Murray said. "How did you know him?"

"I met him yesterday. We must send for the constable."

"Monger?" Auntie said. "The man's an idiot. Send for the justice of the peace. This is a job for McAdam."

"Oh, I think in a case like this you should call the constable," Mrs. Murray said. As the M.P.'s wife, she was allowed to have the final say in the matter.

George—who else?—was sent off for Monger. Mrs. Murray graciously offered the use of her gig for the trip, as Monger has only a donkey cart and the donkey is approaching retirement age.

"I believe we'll continue this reading another time, Mrs. Murray," Aunt Talbot said.

"But my fate line! You were just about to read it."

"I'm too upset to continue this morning. A murder right on our doorstep while we were enjoying ourselves, merry as mice in malt! Gracious me, and Amy and Lollie were talking to him just yesterday."

"Who is he and where did you meet him, Miss Talbot?" Mrs. Murray inquired.

I told her about meeting him while I was sketching.

"Did he say why he was here?" she asked. I was a little surprised that she asked. It seemed she was beginning to assume the proper provincial curiosity. She didn't spend much time in the country. Her being here in May was particularly unusual, with the London Season in full swing.

"He said he was from Bath," Aunt Talbot told her. "Amy caught him out in a black lie. He didn't know a thing about Bath. It's pretty clear the fellow was up to no good."

"But what was he doing here?" Mrs. Murray repeated.

"He said he was on a walking tour," I told her. "Actually, he was looking for relatives in the graveyard. Fanshawe was the name, Rupert and Marion. He said they'd died in the last century. There are no Fanshawes hereabouts other than yourself. You were a Fanshawe before marriage."

She paused a moment. "What did he look like?"

"He was young, tall and thin, with fair hair and blue eyes. He seemed gentlemanly. Very well dressed."

She thought a moment, then shook her head. "No, I don't know him. There are no Stoddarts in my family. Such a pity when a young man dies," she said, rubbing her ugly club thumbs against her fingers. "Well, I was going to take my leave, but since I've lent my gig to your footman . . ."

We did the polite thing and had the horses put to to drive her home.

"I thought she'd never leave," Aunt Talbot exclaimed when the front door closed. "She seemed mighty interested in that corpse, didn't you think?"

"Yes, I noticed she asked twice who he was."

"I believe she was worried about her fate line. I hope I didn't worry her unduly by mentioning it, but there was a noticeable break in her fate line. I judged it to occur near the end of her third decade. It will be a comeuppance for her after having her bread buttered on both sides since her marriage."

I shan't venture into the intricacies of the fate line. Timing its irregularities is a tricky business.

"Let us go down and keep Lollie company," she continued. "It can't be pleasant for him, sitting with a corpse. And there's no saying the murderer won't return."

She was keen to get all the details of the murder firsthand and I was becoming fretful at having left my paint box behind, so I went with her back to the scene of the crime.

Chapter Three

"That there man's been murdered" was Monger's verdict when he beheld the sodden corpse. Monger, a graying man with an undistinguished face and bad teeth, had been a solicitor's clerk until he was dismissed for incompetence, at which time his cousin, McAdam, had appointed him to the post of constable.

"We are not blind, Monger," Aunt Talbot said, glancing at his hands. Despite his earth hands, he displayed nothing outstanding in the way of common sense. "What are you going to do about it?"

"He'll have to be buried" was Monger's reply. "That's not my job."

Auntie has a low tolerance for stupidity. "Send for McAdam, Lollie," she said.

Monger nodded his approval. "Aye, 'twould be best, and a sawbones to give the certificate. There'll be an inquest into this piece of work. I'll sit with the body till Joseph gets here." His cousin, Joseph McAdam.

Aunt Talbot couldn't resist a glance at Stoddart's hands before leaving. "A fire hand, it looks like," she said as an aside. "Unreliable. A revolutionary, I shouldn't wonder."

I recovered my paint box and sketch pad, and we went back across the flower-strewn meadow toward the house. Monger lit up a pipe and sat down on my sketching rock to await McAdam's arrival.

When we had gone beyond hearing, Lollie opened his hand to reveal a waterlogged note. "I got this from Stoddart's pocket," he said. "You just might be right about his being a revolutionary, Aunt Maude."

She flushed with pleasure and forgot to chide him for going through the dead man's pockets. "What does it say, Lollie?"

"Not much, but it looks dashed suspicious. It's printed, for one thing. That hides the handwriting. 'Meet me at the water meadow at six. Bring the money. We'll exchange.' It isn't signed. Stoddart obviously had some agreement with the writer. He knew who the note was from."

"Was there money in his pocket?" Aunt Talbot asked, hastening homeward without breaking stride.

"Not a sou. His watch is gone as well. I noticed he was wearing one yesterday."

Auntie considered this for a moment, then said, "Since the murderer left the note behind when he went through Stoddart's pockets, can we assume that he is not the man who wrote it?"

"The note was folded up and in the bottom of

his watch pocket. If the murderer pulled the watch out by its chain, he'd never have noticed the note."

"An unsigned, printed note doesn't tell us much," I ventured.

"On the contrary," my aunt said. "It tells us a great deal: that Stoddart was buying something clandestinely. Their meeting in the meadow at six in the morning suggests the seller wanted the utmost privacy. And that suggests some manner of illegality."

"The note doesn't say six in the morning," I pointed out. "Perhaps the meeting was for six last night, or tonight, or any night. It might have been in his pocket for days."

Auntie again considered for a moment, then jerked her head in acknowledgment. "Point taken," she said curtly.

"What is more interesting is that the meeting occurred in our water meadow," I said. "Stoddart must have been meeting someone from this neighborhood who would know about it."

"That path through the meadow isn't actually public, but it's used widely by all the locals," Auntie mentioned.

The path she referred to joins two parallel roads. By cutting through the meadow pedestrians can cut a mile from their route. But still, it is only locals who would know about it.

We continued discussing this exciting event after we reached home. We went in by the back door, the closest way. I noticed Cook had George

25

out picking vegetables. Inez had stuck by her vow not to venture out into the garden. Already the effects of the murder were being felt. It seemed almost incredible that a murder should have occurred in this peaceful corner of the land.

George looked up to tell us that the groom was taking Mrs. Murray's gig home and would return in our carriage. One can always count on George to be on top of things. He knew we would want to go to the village ourselves that afternoon.

We sat in the Rose Saloon, each of us keeping one eye turned to the window to watch for McAdam's arrival. Auntie forgot herself so far as to accept a small glass of wine to recover her breath. She sipped at it as if it were hemlock.

Lollie passed around the note, held in place on a plate to keep it from falling apart. It was sodden, but the pulp that remained suggested that it had been a cheap sort of paper. Luckily, the message had been written in pencil. Ink would have run, making the writing illegible.

"A gentleman would have written in ink," Aunt Talbot informed us.

"I wonder what he was exchanging the money for," Lollie said.

"I shouldn't be surprised if he was a spy for Boney, paying for war secrets," Aunt Talbot replied. "Did he have a foreign accent at all?"

"No, not a trace," I said.

"An Englishman, then. A traitor along with all the rest. Never trust a fire hand. I wonder if

McAdam would let me take a print of it. Much the best way to read the lines and mounts."

The print is taken by smearing the hand with ink, placing a clean paper on a sheet of glass, and pressing the hand on the paper. The result is then studied with a magnifying glass to reveal the clues as to the person's character. Even the whorls and loops on the fingertips are examined.

"Don't be a ghoul, Aunt Maude," Lollie scolded.

"His character hardly matters now," she said. "The man is dead. He'll no longer afflict society."

"You're hard on Mr. Stoddart," I said. "Are you forgetting he's the victim? You speak as though he were the murderer."

Auntie looked quite surprised at this. Lollie seemed to have forgotten it as well. I expect it was the man's lying about Bath that had prejudiced their view.

"Perhaps he was an English spy trying to buy French secrets from his murderer," Lollie suggested. He didn't like to admit that an English spy would sink to murder.

"We don't know that it had anything to do with spying or even with that note," I insisted. "It could be that Stoddart was buying stolen goods, or something of that sort."

"A fence," Lollie said, nodding importantly at knowing the cant term. "But I haven't heard of any big robberies hereabouts."

"I wager both men were from London," Aunt Talbot decided. "Much wiser to sell stolen goods away from where they were stolen. What a villain the murderer is, and to think he's running about the countryside, unknown."

She watched from the front window as McAdam rode up on his bay mare, then went to the door to speak to him. When she returned, she said, "He's going directly to the water meadow. No word of any robbery in town. He wants that note, Lollie. It is evidence."

Lollie decided to put it in the oven with the door open to dry it. Unfortunately, Betty closed the door, and it was dark brown by the time the mishap was discovered. When Lollie tried to pick it up, it fell to pieces. McAdam stopped in for a word after viewing the corpus delicti.

McAdam is a short, balding little man with sharp brown eyes. We tease Auntie that he has a *tendre* for her because he once carried her parcels two blocks to the carriage in Chilton Abbas.

We told him all we could remember of our first meeting with Stoddart and of seeing him with Maitland before we spoke to him. He said he'd have a word with Maitland. Lollie told him about finding the body that morning. McAdam chided Lollie for searching the man's pockets and was, of course, not happy to learn the note was now a pile of ashes. Lollie was able to give him the message word for word and even duplicated the printing, which did much to mitigate McAdam's wrath.

That is how we passed the morning. Immediatcly after lunch Auntie remembered she needed a few yards of muslin and put on her bonnet to go to Chilton Abbas. The muslin, of course, was a pretext for going to the drapery shop to retail our adventure to her friends and to learn of any new developments. You have no notion of the importance of gossip in the parish if you imagine for a moment the carriage got away without Lollie and myself in it.

Chilton Abbas is a typical Hampshire village, built around a crystal-clear chalk stream, with a common green complete with duck pond, a High Street, a church, an inn, a tavern, a cluster of shops and houses, and a manor house (occupied by the Murrays) at the end of High Street.

We stabled the carriage at the inn. Lollie went to the tavern and Auntie and I headed to Mulliner's Drapery Shop. We hadn't gone six feet before we were stopped by Mrs. Davis, the vicar's wife and most arrant gossip in the parish.

"I hear you've had a busy morning, Maude!" she exclaimed, her cabbage green eyes aglow.

She invited us in for tea, but Aunt Maude wanted a larger audience and opted for the drapery shop. There, in a dark aisle between the ells of muslin on one side and ribbons and buttons on the other, the ladies of the parish clustered like birds in a treetop, chattering.

Miss Addie Lemon, my particular friend, drew me toward the window. Being unattached ladies, we wanted to keep an eye out for gentlemen passing on the street while we gossiped. I, having firsthand information, opened my budget first. Addie listened eagerly, blue eyes wide open as she gasped and exclaimed at all the proper places.

"Oh, my! What a turn it must have given you. Was it horrid?" And later, "Betty baked the note! Well, I never. What had McAdam to say about that?"

She was not without information of her own to impart. "You heard about the money, of course?"

"Only a mention of it in the note," I replied.

"Five hundred pounds! They say Stoddart had it put in the safe at the inn when he first arrived, then late yesterday afternoon he took it out. He didn't leave the money in his room, for McAdam searched it from top to bottom and there wasn't a sou in it."

"Were there guests staying at the inn?"

"No one suspicious. They say there was a cock-fight in an abandoned barn last night and Stoddart was there, along with half the men from the neighborhood. He might have lost the money on a bet. But it's only a rumor, mind. Oh, and there's been a stranger spotted about town. A tall, dark gentleman. Someone says he was seen talking to Stoddart." Such vague *on-dits* were only to be expected. I paid little heed to them.

We were so engrossed in our conversation, we nearly missed Maitland. It was Addie who spotted him first, heading toward the drapery shop. We knew he would not enter that female den and began primping our hair. We managed to be leaving the shop just as he passed by.

"Ladies," he said, lifting his curled beaver and bowing.

Morris Maitland is so marvelous a creature, I can never quite make up my mind what part of him to admire first. The sun glinted off a golden wave of hair that fell forward when he removed his hat. His blue eyes shone like sapphires; his teeth sparkled. Maitland in the flesh always outdid memory. His blue superfine jacket hugged his broad shoulders. His buckskins were spotless, and little gold tassels bobbed on his gleaming topboots.

Addie overcame her breathlessness first. "Miss Talbot was just telling me you know Mr. Stoddart, the man who was murdered," she said.

Maitland gave me a mock frown. "So it is you I have to thank for McAdam's call," he said. "I would hardly say I know him. I caught him trespassing on my property yesterday morning. He explained that he was out walking and lost his way. We shared a cheroot and he told me about a boxing match he'd seen in Winchester." This jibed with what Stoddart had told us.

"He didn't mention that he was looking for his relatives' graves?" I asked.

After a frowning pause, Maitland said, "I believe he did ask the way to the graveyard. He mentioned he was from Bath. I have relatives there myself, but he didn't happen to know any of them."

"That would be because he wasn't from Bath," I informed him.

Maitland's eyebrows rose. "Is he not? I'm sure he said Bath. . . ."

"Oh, yes, he *said* Bath, but I doubt he'd ever been there. He knew nothing of the place."

"Where was he from?" Maitland asked.

"I have no idea."

"Did you hear about the money?" Addie asked him.

He hadn't, and she had the pleasure of telling him. Not to be outdone, I told him about the note. He displayed a suitable degree of interest in both stories. Addie mentioned her theory regarding the cockfight. Maitland admitted he had been there and said he had not seen Stoddart. Altogether, we monopolized Maitland for quite ten minutes, to the consternation of the other village maidens. Before leaving, he inquired if we planned to attend the spring assembly and asked us both to save him a dance.

We returned to the drapery shop in a state of high elation and bought new ribbons to impress Maitland at the next assembly. Mrs. Davis invited Auntie and myself for tea again and we accepted this time. As we were to meet Lollie at four-thirty, we could not remain long.

We were home by five. We neither had company nor went out that evening. I did some painting and went to bed early. As I lay in the dark, I thought of Stoddart, who would soon be moldering in the ground. He hadn't seemed like a spy or an evil man. Pretending he was from Bath wasn't reason enough to be murdered.

I knew Lollie planned to involve himself in the case, and I decided that I'd do anything I could to help him.

Chapter Four

With a murderer in our midst, I decided to do my sketching close to home the next morning. Lollie was busy about the estate and we couldn't spare George to accompany me. I was just strolling through the park with my sketch pad and watercolor box trying to decide what to sketch when I heard the clatter of hooves. Looking through the trees to the road, I saw our neighbor, Beau Sommers, was coming to call. Another gentleman was with him.

Five years ago the sight of Beau would have sent my heart racing in delight. At a callow seventeen I could imagine no greater enchantment than a kind word from Beau. His curled lip and air of cynicism had seemed the height of sophistication to me. Now that I have some small experience of men and the world, I recognize him for what he is. A gazetted flirt, a fribble, a here-and-thereian who gives each new generation of ladies a fling as they put up their hair and let down their skirts.

I had my innoculation at seventeen. He still calls from time to time, when he is in the suds and fears he may need my dowry. I expect when he is about forty he will marry some youngster for the sake of an heir, but I doubt he will ever provide his lady with a tame husband. He is tall and well enough built, with dark hair and brown eyes. The cut of his jacket and the arrangement of his cravat are of more importance to him than the profitable management of his estate, Beauvert.

When he espied me, he and his friend came forward and dismounted to greet me. I suspected at a glance that Beau's friend was cast from the same mold as himself. The fashionable cut of his blue jacket of Bath cloth and the intricate folds of his cravat suggested it. He wore his curled beaver at the same cocky angle, tilted over a lean, tanned face. Like Beau, he rode a prime blood bay. And, like Beau, his eyes examined me with a purely physical interest.

"Miss Amy," Beau said, lifting his hat. For a period of two weeks five years ago he had called me Amy. Miss Amy was the compromise he settled on, halfway between the formal Miss Talbot and the friendlier Amy. Its unsuitability didn't bother Beau. I have no elder sister; I am Miss Talbot to my acquaintances, Amy to my friends.

"Good morning, Beau," I replied, not because I wanted to foster any intimacy, but because everyone called him Beau. I had done so for years.

"May I present Mr. Renshaw, an old chum

from university." Beau had attended Oxford for one year.

Renshaw lifted his lids, bowed, smiled a well-practiced smile, and said in a bored drawl, "Charmed, Miss Talbot. Beau has been singing your praises so loudly, I insisted he introduce me." His eyes toured from my head to toes and back up again while I scarcely had time to glance at him. Yet I felt I had been thoroughly assessed as a physical specimen in that brief second.

The first thing I noticed when he removed his hat was a scar above his left eyebrow. The white scar, shaped like the blade of a scythe, stood out against his swarthy skin. His dark eyes were hooded, giving him a lazy look, as if he were still half asleep. His thin lips curved in a cool smile. He would have been more handsome without that theatrical air of ennui. His build, I noticed, was impressive. His well-cut jacket sat easily on his broad shoulders. His buckskins lay flat against a firm stomach.

"How do you do," I said coolly, and offered him my hand. Being caught in midbow, he looked at it as if he didn't quite know what to do with it but finally took it and gave it a limp shake.

"Now you see for yourself I spoke no more than the truth," Beau said to his chum. They both gazed at me with feigned admiration, as if I were Helen of Troy. I knew I looked a sight in my dowdy painting gown and an old straw bonnet. I began to suspect that one of them had an eye on my dowry. "Did you ever see such eyes, Renny?"

Renshaw murmured unconvincingly of sapphires and cornflowers.

"I assume you're referring to cornflower leaves, Mr. Renshaw," I said. "My eyes are green."

He had the grace to blush at that, before casting an irritated glance at his cohort. Had Beau told him I had blue eyes? Was he blind, that he couldn't see for himself they were green?

"Miss Amy would know all about flowers and leaves," Beau said. "Did I mention she is a consummate artist? She paints weeds."

"Wildflowers," I corrected with my own tinge of irritation.

"May we see what you've been sketching, Miss Talbot?" Renshaw asked, glancing at my sketch pad.

"I shall have a word with your aunt while you show Renshaw your pictures," Beau said, thus inviting himself into the house. The gentlemen exchanged a conspiratorial look.

I either had to ask them both in or remain alone with Renshaw. When I saw the small, predatory smile settle on Renshaw's lips, I felt vaguely threatened and said, "Won't you both come inside?"

"Too kind," Renshaw said, swallowing his annoyance.

Beau carried my paint box. They walked their mounts up the roadway, where the gardener's helper took the horses around to the stable. Beau spoke of the murder. It was the main topic of conversation in every local household that day.

"I hear you and Lollie actually found the body," he said. "What an unpleasant experience! And I wager you didn't even have a bottle of hartshorn in your paint box."

"Oddly enough, I went out without it that morning." I replied. I thought Renshaw's lips quirked at my reply, but I couldn't be sure. He turned his head aside just then.

Once we were in the saloon, Beau made a great fuss over Auntie, telling her she looked younger every time he saw her and suggesting that hard work must be good for ladies.

"I manage to keep busy," she allowed.

"The devil finds work for idle hands. Have you read any good palms lately, Miss Talbot?" he inquired, as if hands were books.

"There is no such thing as a bad palm, Mr. Sommers. One must not blame the gun for killing the hare. The palm, like the gun, is but the instrument. Hands are the mirrors of the soul. They only reflect what is within."

Renshaw's air of ennui changed to mild interest. His lazy eyes opened wider. "Except in the case of the left hand, surely. The left hand indicates what you were born with. The right hand is what you have made of your inherited tendencies."

"Very true," Auntie said, moving her chair a notch closer to his. "Except in the case of left-handed folks, when the reverse holds true."

"What is your view on the reading of people who are ambidextrous, Miss Talbot?" he inquired.

I examined him suspiciously, finding it odd that a fashionable fribble should be interested in palmistry. He appeared to be perfectly serious.

"Everyone favors one hand or the other," she stated categorically. "When in doubt I toss the subject a ball of wool. Whichever hand he puts up to catch it is his dominant hand. He had only trained his passive hand to do his bidding."

"That's very interesting! I was of the opinion that whichever hand was happier holding a pen was the deciding factor."

"But then there are people who can write equally well with either hand," she pointed out. "Take Mr. Majors now, the solicitor's son-in-law."

The two palmists discussed their avocation for a few minutes. I was not disappointed, but I was just a little surprised that Renshaw paid no attention whatsoever to myself. It was not long before tea was ordered. I saw that Renshaw was going to be a welcome addition to Auntie's circle. But as we were waiting for the tea, he made the error of offering his hand for a reading and he fell from favor.

"Oh, dear, a fire hand!" Auntie exclaimed.

Long palm, short fingers. Renshaw was nothing else but a bustling busybody, a show-off, volatile and bad-tempered. There is little good to be said of a fire hand. It is the pariah of hands.

Even the fine emerald on the smallest finger of his left hand couldn't save him.

I could see plainly that Renshaw was frustrated by his fall from grace. He looked a question at Beau, who hunched his shoulders. It was then I began to suspect Renshaw's interest in palmistry was assumed, to make himself welcome at Oakbay. I could see no conceivable advantage to ingratiating himself with my aunt except to have access to the house—and to me. Definitely he had designs on my dowry and was devious enough to have invented this ploy to make himself welcome.

After the tea arrived, the subject of palm reading was forgotten.

"It is odd Mr. Sommers hasn't brought you to call before, Mr. Renshaw, as you are such old friends," my aunt said.

"Renny has been in India, working with the East India Company," Beau explained.

"That's very interesting," she said. "I have a brother with the E.I.C. He doesn't actually work in India. He is with the administration office in London. Whereabouts were you stationed in India?"

"In Calcutta," Renshaw replied. "I was acting as liaison between the head office and the office in Calcutta."

"Perhaps you know my brother, Hillary Talbot?"

After a frowning pause, Renshaw said, "I've seen the name on letters, but I haven't met him."

He spoke on a little about the heat and

monsoons and markets and such things as everyone back from India mentions.

"A man can do very well for himself in India," Auntie said in a considering way. Her eyes slid to me. Fire hand or not, a nabob might provide a husband. If a water hand couldn't control fire, what could?

"It is the nawabs who make the colossal fortunes you hear of, ma'am," he told her. "I have returned to England to make my fortune."

I own I was surprised that he admitted to a lack of fortune. That was no way to make himself welcome at Oakbay.

Beau laughed, a high, unnatural laugh. "Why, you are giving the ladies the notion you're a pauper, Renny." Then he added to my aunt, "Renny's papa left him a very tidy estate in Kent. A hop farm. That is why he returned from Calcutta."

Renshaw tried to look modest.

"I expect you'll be returning to Kent very soon to look after your business," she said.

"Yes, very soon. Having been away from England for so long, I wanted to look up my old friends first."

"I shouldn't waste too much time if I were you. An estate doesn't run itself. It has to be watched over closely."

"I have a steward, but I plan to return soon. There is one cousin in particular I want to see. I have a message for him from a lady in India.

An affair of the heart. I heard he was on a walking tour in this part of the country."

"A walking tour, you say?" I asked, thinking, of course, of Stoddart. "What was his name?"

"Matthew Bennet. Why, have you . . ."

"No, I'm afraid I don't recognize the name." He looked at me with sharp interest, as if waiting for me to say more.

"I've convinced Renny to stay with me until the assembly on the weekend," Beau said. "There is no saying, Matthew might show up."

Beau engaged my aunt in some local gossip and Renshaw turned to me. "You were going to show me your sketches, Miss Talbot," he said.

The pad I had been carrying was a new one. It had nothing in it except the few sketches I had made at the water meadow and the loosestrife in the orchard. I opened the book and showed him the fritillary. The composition was lopsided. I had drawn it on the left side of the page, leaving space for other sketches of the flower as it opened and faded.

"This is only a sketch. It still has to be painted properly and finished in pen," I said. It looked a poor enough thing in its unfinished state, but Mr. Renshaw found a few compliments.

"Very natural, lifelike," he said, and turned the page to view the monkeyflower. He owned he had seen flowers very like it but had never known their name. Then he turned the page and I heard a sharp intake of breath.

Looking at the page, I saw my sketch of Stoddart. In the excitement of the murder I had forgotten all about it.

"Who—who is this?" Renshaw asked. He had suddenly lost his bored drawl. The eyes staring at me were intelligent, alert.

I told him. "You sounded very surprised when you saw the sketch, Mr. Renshaw," I said, looking a question at him. "It isn't your missing cousin, is it?" My unspoken thought was that his cousin might have been using an alias, if he were up to something illegal.

"No. My surprise was to see a human face amidst the wildflowers. I didn't realize you did people. I was expecting a daisy and saw this *superb* sketch. It's really quite marvelous." He studied it, tilting his head this way and that. "Almost a touch of da Vinci, the way you've shaded in the eyes and mouth."

Naturally I was flattered to death at this comparison. When I first began sketching, I wanted to do portraits, but my skill wasn't up to the task. When I discovered wildflowers, I knew I had found my calling, but I am still a great admirer of Leonardo's. Lady Hadley has a few of his cartoons, which she was kind enough to show me. The shading, in particular, is so subtle that it can quite bring a face alive. There is no definable boundary between the highlight and the shade in those sketches. One blends into the other with such infinite finesse that it is almost magic. My hasty sketch had none of this artistry, but I flushed with pleasure and began to think that Renshaw was really quite handsome.

"Who is the man?" he asked in a casual tone.

"That is the unfortunate victim, Mr. Stoddart. I met him in the water meadow the day before he was killed."

Renshaw expressed interest and I told him all about that one meeting with Stoddart, who was looking for his relatives' graves, and so on.

"Well, it is certainly a marvelous sketch," he said. "I shall know where to come to have my portrait painted for the family gallery."

"I don't work in oils, Mr. Renshaw. Indeed, I seldom paint people at all except for the family."

"Pity. Mama has been after me to have my likeness taken. I should like to send her a sketch, a charcoal perhaps, for her birthday. You wouldn't consider it . . ." His dark eyes were fully open now.

"Mrs. Bliss, in Chilton Abbas, could do a better job for you," I said, not quite closing the door on doing it myself.

"Will you give me another chance to convince you?" he asked in a flirtatious way. "I brought my curricle with me and my team of grays. Sixteen miles an hour. Beau is busy this afternoon and I planned to drive into the village. I would appreciate having someone from the neighborhood to show me the sights."

I had nothing planned for the afternoon and thought it might be amusing to have a fling in his carriage. "Very well," I agreed after a suitable pause to show maidenly reluctance.

"You are excessively kind, ma'am," he said.

We agreed on an hour and the gentlemen soon left.

"I wonder what brought Sommers down on our heads," Aunt Talbot said, setting the cups back on the tray. The devil would be hard put to find *her* hands idle. "He doesn't seem to be dangling after you this time. What did you think of young Renshaw?"

"I thought he was quite nice. I've agreed to show him around the village this afternoon."

She looked at me as if I had grown horns. "You're going out with a complete stranger, and a friend of Beau Sommers to boot? Are you insane? He might be the murderer, for all we know."

"Oh, I hardly think so, Auntie. He didn't recognize Stoddart at all when I showed him the sketch. Besides, he only arrived at Beau's this morning."

"I noticed him emptying the butter boat on you. I expect that hop farm he's come into is next door to bankrupt. A dowry of fifteen thousand would be useful."

"I shall insist on visiting it before handing him my dowry, in the unlikely event that he offers marriage while we are driving into Chilton Abbas. Goose! It is only a drive. Is there anything you need in the village?"

She decided to try to get up a whist game for

that evening and went to write up her notes for me to deliver. I went back outdoors and did a sketch of some red clover that grows in the park.

I teased Auntie about her concern for me, but I would heed her warning all the same. Any friend of Beau Sommers's automatically fell under suspicion of being no better than he should be. I remembered the conspiratorial look Beau and Renshaw had exchanged when I invited them inside. Had this been their plan from the beginning, to set Renshaw up for a date with me? He would not find me easy plucking, if it was my fortune he had in his eye.

Chapter Five

"Aunt Maude tells me that you have a new beau," Lollie said over lunch. "If it's the fellow I saw driving toward Beauvert this morning, I wouldn't mind having a go in his curricle someday. A bang-up rattler and prads. Sixteen miles an hour, I warrant."

"What time did you see him?" my aunt asked.

"Around seven. I saw him from my bedroom window as I was dressing. He was heading toward Beauvert."

"Coming from the east?"

"Yes. Why?"

"Because it sounds like Mr. Renshaw, who's

from Kent. The fellow is visiting Sommers. He says he arrived this morning. If he's telling the truth, he must have driven all night. Mind you, his eyes *were* half closed."

"I can't imagine anyone being that keen to see Beau," Lollie said, spearing a thick slice of ham and slathering on the mustard. "Why is he here?"

I told him about Renshaw's being home from India, looking up old friends.

"Very strange, his arriving on the heels of the murder" was Aunt Talbot's opinion. The words "fire hand" hung, unspoken, on the air.

"If you think he's a wrong 'un, write to Uncle Hillary," Lollie suggested. "He'd know if Renshaw has picked up a bad aroma in India. Knows all the fellows they send out there. That's what his job is, handling recruits."

"That's an idea," Aunt Talbot said. She writes to Uncle Hillary once a month. As she had just mailed her monthly letter a week ago, I didn't think she would write again so soon, unless Renshaw showed greater interest in my dowry.

Lollie had left before the mail arrived and flipped through his mail as he ate. "A dun from Millar," he said. "I suppose I ought to pay him for those topboots I got last December. I shall visit the bank after lunch and pay our local accounts."

Auntie mentioned that she would go through the linen cupboard that afternoon to see what required mending or replacing. She was upstairs at that chore when Renshaw arrived, and as we were leaving at once, I didn't have her called downstairs but just picked up my bonnet. The mirror in the front hall is shadowed by a potted palm and it depresses me to see myself in it, looking like a ghost. I took my bonnet into the morning parlor, which has a friendly light. Practicality told me I should wear a plain round bonnet in an open carriage, but I felt Renshaw's exquisite jacket merited better and had chosen my second best, a low poke with a modest feather. Renshaw stepped in behind me.

While I tied on my bonnet in front of the mirror, he said, "I see you have wisely chosen a plain bonnet. I meant to caution you to do so."

I saw at once that our notions of fashion were at odds. "A plain bonnet," indeed!

He strolled away from the mirror to examine a series of six of my paintings that hung on the wall. Their subject was fruit: a pineapple cut in half, showing the juicy center; a pair of lemons with the leaves still attached; a cluster of green grapes; and so on. The framer had done an excellent job. The narrow mahogany frames suited the modest room. A mat of dark green added contrast to the light paper I had used. Since they were pictures of fruit, I had put them in the small dining room. They hung along the length of one wall, forming, I thought, a pretty little gallery.

"But these are marvelous!" Renshaw exclaimed in accents of surprise. "So lifelike, the texture of that pineapple! I can almost taste it."

They were rather good, but why should that

surprise him when he had compared my work to Leonardo's? "Thank you," I said.

Renshaw must have noticed the curious tone of my voice. It was hard to discover a blush beneath his swarthy skin, but he looked as if he was blushing.

He said sheepishly, "Not that it surprises me! I had thought, when I saw your other nature sketches, that your true métier was the human face, but I see now that you excel in both fields."

"Those were preliminary sketches. There's still a great deal of work to be done on them. I'm glad you like my fruit paintings."

"They really are wonderful, Miss Talbot." I sensed real admiration, or perhaps I was only hearing what I wanted to hear. "How I would love to have such a talent."

"Let us hope your talent lies with cultivating hops," I suggested playfully.

"Hops?" he asked, frowning in confusion. "Oh, you refer to my inheritance. Yes, one can only hope, but I meant an artistic talent. Everyone needs a creative outlet. I confess, I'm not much acquainted with hops yet, except in ale, of course."

"You took no interest in your papa's work before you left England?"

He looked surprised at the question. I felt he wasn't accustomed to sensible conversation from a lady, but he answered readily enough.

"Youngsters are too foolish for such things," he said. "I was away at school and university, you know, then I went to India when I was still a young cub.''

I knew what he meant. Lollie had shown no interest in farming until Papa died and he took over the reins of Oakbay.

We went out to his curricle. It was what Lollie would call a smasher: an awesome vehicle, gleaming a brilliant yellow in the sunlight, with silver appointments glinting. I felt as dashing as Lettie Lade when he boosted me up into the high seat. Heads would turn in Chilton Abbas when we went racing through town.

He certainly set a lively pace on the open road before we reached town. He was a fine fiddler, driving quickly but never giving rise to fear. Once we arrived, however, he slowed to half the speed, which greatly diminished the effect and the danger to pedestrians. It was the proper thing to do, but it was not what Beau Sommers would have done, nor any of his usual friends, either. I began to reconsider my first opinion of Renshaw.

I mentioned that I had Auntie's invitations to deliver, but first we took one turn along the High Street to impress the locals.

''We won't have to go in at each house and chat, will we?'' he asked.

''Are you in a hurry to get home, Mr. Renshaw?''

''Not at all. I'm in a hurry to get back out on the open road and give the horses their heads. I just bought this team and carriage. They're still a novelty to me.''

If he was after my fortune, he would have said he wanted to be alone with me. And if he was not after my fortune, why had he come to call? Why had he asked me out? I was beginning to feel a real interest in Beau's mysterious guest.

"How long have you been home from India?" I asked.

"Two weeks. I've had the team for one."

"In that case, I shall leave each note with the servant at the door and say I am in a great rush."

He smiled a lazy smile. "Kind as well as talented—and beautiful." My suspicions stirred at this speech. "Even if your eyes aren't sapphires." He winced in memory. "That was ill done of me. And to say it to an artist, of all people, one who is finely attuned to shades. You must have thought me a jackass."

"No, only disinterested. I expect Beau told you I had blue eyes."

"He did, as he told me you drew weeds. 'Dashed odd filly,' he called you." He smiled to lessen the sting.

I could just hear Beau saying that in his querulous tone. "Then why did you come to call?"

"I am just back from India. I wanted to meet all the pretty ladies."

I mentally translated that to "eligible ladies." "I shall introduce you to the local ladies at the assembly," I said.

His lips opened in a teasing smile. "Tired of me so soon, Miss Talbot?"

"Have you forgotten so soon that I'm kind? It would be selfish of me to keep you all to myself."

"Kind, talented—and a minx. Oh, and I forgot—beautiful. What an intriguing combination. And here Beau assured me you were the veriest provincial. Did I mention that?"

"You left that compliment out. Odd you were so eager to meet me, in that case."

"Oh, but I adore provincials. You mustn't mistake me for a town buck."

My eyes toured his jacket, handsome cravat, and York tan gloves. "It is clear to the most untrained eye that you have no interest in fashion," I said ironically.

"That is exactly what my London friends said when they saw what I wore home from Calcutta. You will notice my clothes, like my curricle, are new. As I plan to keep them for some time, I invested in the best. Quality pays in the long run. Where do we take the first invitation?"

Mrs. Davis was the closest recipient. She came hastening to the door and kept me chatting for five minutes, while peering over my shoulder at Renshaw and asking a hundred questions about him.

"Sorry," I said when I finally got back to Renshaw. "But it's all your own fault. You can't expect to drive such a flashy rig as this and not have everyone inquiring about you."

It was three-quarters of an hour later before we got out of town. Besides delivering the notes, we were stopped by a half-dozen friends and then we met Lollie.

He came pouncing forward to greet not me or Renshaw but the curricle and the grays. After admiring every glint of silver and every point of the team, he said, "By the way, sis, can you change a tenner for me? I want to pay the cobbler, but he doesn't have change for a ten."

"I don't carry that much money on me!"

"Perhaps I can help," Renshaw said, and drew out a pretty thick purse. He gave Lollie two fives. As he took Lollie's ten-pound note, I noticed that he examined it in a careful but surreptitious way. He looked at the front, then turned it over.

"It ain't a forgery," Lollie said, ready to take offense.

Renshaw looked up and grinned. "Nothing personal, Talbot. Didn't you hear there are forged notes about? Very good ones, I hear. Beau got one last night in a game of cards. As you said you just came from the bank, I was concerned that you might have been given one in error, but this one is genuine right enough."

He showed us how the forged notes could be recognized by some irregularity of the printing on the back of the note.

"I shall be on the lookout for that," Lollie said. "Thank you for warning me, Renshaw."

"As your money is good, you are welcome to join us in a game of roulette at Beau's place tonight."

Lollie's eyes lit up like a lamp. "By Jove!"

"Auntie is counting on you to fill in at her card table this evening, Lollie," I said at once. I was happy to have an excuse at hand. Beau's games were for high stakes and Lollie is a mere tyro at gambling.

"Dash it, who wants to play with a bunch of old ladies?"

"It will not all be old ladies. She invited the Lemons as well. Addie will be coming."

"Another time, Talbot," Renshaw said, and won favor by adding, "You must try the reins of my grays one day soon."

"By Jove!" Lollie said again. He soon left, promising to be in touch with Renshaw to arrange a mutually satisfactory day and hour for testing the grays.

"That was demmed thoughtless of me," Renshaw said at once. He looked genuinely sorry. "I take it, from your quick intervention, that you don't like your brother gambling."

"The best throw of the dice is to throw them away." That was one of Auntie's proverbs. When I noticed Renshaw's lips twitching in amusement at such an antiquated attitude, I added, "Beau's games are for high stakes. Lollie is only eighteen years old, Mr. Renshaw. Not quite ready to tangle with the likes of Beau."

Renshaw sighed. "I can see Beau has changed somewhat from the days when I knew him. I had hoped to see him settled down—married—but he seems strangely restless. It's interesting, renewing acquaintances with old friends after so many years."

"I don't think Beau is in any hurry to settle down."

"The more fool he," Renshaw said.

I looked to see if he was being ironic. He looked only rueful. Was it possible Renshaw was truly interested in marriage as apart from nabbing an heiress?

We were talking in the carriage. Before we got away, Addie Lemon spotted us and came forward to meet Renshaw.

"I can't expect to cause any fuss at the assembly at this rate," he complained in mock annoyance after she had left. "I'll be as well known as an old ballad."

"Do you not improve on longer acquaintance?" I asked.

My question was greeted with a challenging, confident smile. "You tell me, ma'am. This is the second time we've met. Am I even more tedious than the first time?"

Such self-confidence required a good setdown. "That would be impossible, Mr. Renshaw," I said demurely.

"Cut to the quick, wretch!" he exclaimed, clutching a hand to his heart. Then he laughed. "That will teach me to go fishing for compliments in a dry stream."

"The stream is not dry, sir. You are merely using the wrong bait."

He examined me with interest. "Can you suggest a more successful bait, Miss Talbot?"

"Surely it is not for the prey to advise the predator, but you must not take the notion I am a gudgeon only because I happen to live in the backwaters of the country."

"You're hard on me. I am only seeking your approval, a kind word . . ."

I found myself becoming intrigued by Renshaw in spite of my aunt's warning. Everything about the man suggested wealth and privilege. His jackets, the emerald on his finger, the team and sporting carriage—all were of the first stare. His manner, too, was easy without being insinuating. Best of all, he could laugh at himself.

Yet by his own admission his career in India had not been distinguished. It was not gentlemen of wealth and privilege who were sent to India but younger sons with their way to make in the world. Renshaw must have known he would inherit his papa's estate. Why had he gone to India at all? Perhaps the hop farm was small. The only other explanation I could think of was that he had been escaping some scandal. That was easy enough to believe of any friend of Beau's.

But if there had been a scandal a decade ago I felt Renshaw had changed. He spoke almost wistfully of settling down, marrying. Unless, of course, it was all an act. He had either been acting when I first met him or he was acting now.

To lead the conversation toward India, I asked,

"Was it in India that you became interested in palmistry, Mr. Renshaw?"

He glanced at me with a perfectly frank expression. "No, Miss Talbot, it was in Hampshire, when Beau told me your aunt is a devotee. I try to make myself agreeable to strangers. Your aunt had read Beau's palm and he briefed me on a few points. Pity he hadn't remembered the significance of a fire hand."

"You're very frank!"

"I am coming to the conclusion that there is no point in trying to con you, ma'am. Those green eyes see too much."

"Why should you want to con me or, indeed, anyone? Surely that is not the way to make yourself agreeable to new acquaintances."

"That is a perfect example of what I mean. Here are we, a fairly handsome young couple, driving in a new curricle with a spirited team on a lovely spring day and you refuse to feel romantic. You insist on talking common sense."

"It takes two to talk sense, Mr. Renshaw. Why should you want to con me?"

"It also takes two to flirt, Miss Talbot. Why do *you* refuse to flirt? I am eligible—by which we both understand my pockets aren't to let. I have a good character. My face may not set every heart aflutter, but taking into account the spring season I had hoped for something more than mere common sense."

"I take leave to tell you, Mr. Renshaw, that

you are a weasel. I repeat, why should you want to con me?"

"And you, ma'am, are a badger. I was not trying to con you. Any bachelor will tell you the way to a young lady's heart—or at least company—is via her chaperone. Beau said your aunt was 'crusty' and suggested she was not vulnerable to compliments but to an interest in palmistry. You see what a deal of trouble I've been to, only to get you into my carriage. And what thanks do I get? Common sense. Nothing but common sense. Really, Miss Renshaw, I expected better of an *artiste*."

That explanation was a mite too flattering to swallow holus-bolus, but I knew I would get nothing better from this prevaricator. "Pity Beau hadn't warned you of the danger of a fire hand," I said.

"Next time I shall read the tea leaves and give your aunt back for that estimate of my character."

"Oh, are you taking Auntie to tea? She didn't mention it."

He emitted a long, exasperated sigh. We drove a few miles east of Chilton Abbas, then he turned the curricle around and we drove back toward Oakbay Hall. I picked up the whip, just fiddling with it to give my hands something to do. Taking into account our delays in the village, it had been a long enough drive for a first outing. I expected we would go directly home. But as we passed the church, Renshaw drew off the road and stopped.

"The water meadow where you did your

sketches is behind the church, I think you mentioned?"

I hadn't mentioned it, but he might have learned it from Beau. "Yes."

"It sounds fascinating. Could we have a look at it?"

I felt a shiver to even think of that place. Yet it held a fascination as well as repugnance. I wouldn't go there alone for some time, but I felt safe with Renshaw.

"Very well, but there is not much to see."

"I think you mentioned a graveyard . . . That is 'a fine and private place/But none, I think, do there embrace.'" He came to a dead stop. "Oh, Lord! What an *asinine* thing to say! You'll think I'm planning to misbehave. I promise you I am not. The lines are from a poem."

I looked at the whip, thinking it would provide a weapon—not if Renshaw misbehaved. I wasn't really concerned about that. But if the murderer had returned to the scene of the crime . . .

"You shan't need that. Word of a gentleman," he said, and removed the whip from my fingers. Setting it aside, he alit and helped me down from the high seat of the curricle.

Chapter Six

There is some enchantment in a water meadow. The atmosphere is so soft and moist. The very air looks green from the surrounding trees and grass. Light from the water plays on the vegetation, giving a magical sense of movement to the stillness. On arrival, all seems silent, but if you stop a moment and listen, there is a veritable symphony of nearly inaudible sounds. The buzz of insects, the rustle of a leaf as it is moved by the breeze, an occasional chirp of a bird, and the louder splash as a frog leaps for a gnat.

As my eyes toured the greenery for a likely candidate for sketching in the future, I forgot Renshaw for a moment. When he spoke, I gave a little leap of surprise.

"It's very peaceful here," he said. There was a tinge of reverence in his tone, the sort of hushed voice one hears in church. I sensed that he appreciated the simple beauty of my outdoor cathedral and liked him better for it. He spied a snakehead and went toward it. "This must be where you were sketching," he said.

"No, it was farther to the right."

He went along and found the very plant I had sketched the day we met Stoddart, close to the spot where Lollie had found his body the next day. I noticed Renshaw peering into the bulrushes beyond. I knew what he was thinking.

"That's where my brother found the body," I said.

"Is all this your land, Miss Talbot?"

"The water meadow separates our land from Mr. Maitland's. The property line runs down the center."

His eyes gazed across the water, up the incline, and soon discovered the shepherd's hut. When I mentioned that Lollie and I had seen Stoddart there with Maitland, nothing would do but Renshaw must see it. And I was just curious enough that I went along with him.

There was little enough to see. The sod hut, with its perishing thatched roof, was a square of six or seven feet on all sides. The only opening was the doorway. As the place had been abandoned for years, any creature comforts had been removed. All that remained was a bed of straw in one corner. Renshaw made straight for it.

"This is new straw!" he exclaimed.

A pile of fresh straw had been placed on top of the old. "I expect some tramp has spent the night here. Perhaps that is how poor Mr. Stoddart was killed," I suggested.

Renshaw lifted up the new top straw and examined it. Then he lifted something out and held it up. It was a length of a lady's blue ribbon about a foot long. There is nothing much to distinguish one blue ribbon from another. There must be two dozen local ladies who wore ribbons similar to the one Renshaw held between his thumb and finger. In fact, Mrs. Murray had been wearing blue ribbons yesterday when Aunt Talbot was reading her palm.

"It seems the tramp got lucky," Renshaw said.

I gave him a cool stare for this piece of impropriety. "You aren't in India now, Mr. Renshaw. Indian manners aren't appreciated here."

"You do the Indians an injustice. They are extremely polite. But not even they are so polite as to honor a vagrant in the manner this ribbon suggests."

"It's perfectly obvious some serving girl has been meeting her beau here," I said, displeased with this broad talk.

He handed me the ribbon. "Very nice ribbon for a serving maid," he said.

It was a satin ribbon, richer than could be purchased in Chilton Abbas. Mulliner's keeps a thin, skimpy satin ribbon. Not narrow in width, but flimsy. It soon loses its shape. The shade of this ribbon was also richer than could be had locally. And there was a hint of purple in it, sort of a periwinkle shade.

"Ladies often give their older ribbons to their servants," I said. "I trust you aren't suggesting a lady was using the hut for a trysting spot."

"So far as I know there are no ladies living on this property. Maitland is a bachelor, is he not?"

"Yes. And before you say it, Mr. Renshaw, I am the lady living closest to the hut. I assure you

61

I did not—" His startled stare told me I had defended my fair name unnecessarily.

"I never suspected it for a moment. You stand much too high on your dignity, ma'am. What I am wondering is whether you happened to give this ribbon to one of your servants."

"I did not. A lady with green eyes doesn't usually wear blue ribbons."

He dangled the bit of ribbon by my face. "It would look well with your hair, though," he said. I jerked my head away. "Well, well. I believe we have a clue here," he said, and folding the ribbon up, he put it in his pocket.

"You should give it to McAdam."

He ignored my suggestion. "While we're here, shall we have a look at the graveyard?" he said.

"I've had enough of an outing for one day, but as you are so interested in Mr. Stoddart's murder, the graves he was looking for belonged to the Fanshawes. There're no such graves in our cemetery."

We began the walk back to the carriage, with the graveyard looming ahead on our right.

"I own I'm intrigued by this murder," he admitted. "What could be serious enough for one human being to kill another—outside of the folly of war, I mean?"

"I believe you'll find man's ego is usually the cause. As you have just come from India, I'm sure you've seen examples of it." He looked a question at me. "I'm referring to suttee, the delightful notion men have that their widows should hop on the funeral pyre and join them in the hereafter."

"Why, that is really a compliment to the ladies, ma'am. Their spouses can't do without them even in the afterlife."

"A high price to pay for a compliment! If it is the wife who dies first, the husband doesn't repay in kind. He manages to get along very well—with another wife."

"It's a cruel custom, but you can't lay it in my dish, Miss Talbot. It was done long before I went to India and will no doubt continue now that I've left. In fact, I've never seen it myself. Each society has its own customs that often seem bizarre to outsiders. The French eat frogs; we eat cows; the Indians immolate their widows."

"The customs are hardly comparable!"

"I doubt a cow would see the difference. They're God's creatures, too." He scowled at me and added, "And, yes, I do eat beef."

"I didn't ask!"

I was surprised he didn't mention that the English were trying to ban suttee. Uncle Hillary had more than once spoken hotly on the subject. The Raj was dead set against suttee.

"You're probably right to suggest man's ego was at the root of the murder, however," he allowed. "A blow to his purse or his pride— either one could be the reason. Perhaps a lady is involved."

"It's not usually ladies who murder."

"Not by means of stabbing, at least, though I

don't acquit the fair sex of deadly passion," he said. "It's more usual for a lady to use poison. But I said only involved—as the cause, was my meaning."

When I didn't reply, he said, "All right-thinking men cherish their wives above rubies, you must know. To have a wife stolen demands some extraordinary revenge."

"The same revenge that's customarily exacted when a man cheats at cards, in fact."

"Or is sold a jade disguised as a goer," he added, failing to acknowledge my point.

"Why do you assume Mr. Stoddart stole some man's wife? He didn't strike me as that sort."

"Unflirtable, was he?"

"He seemed nice. If a lady was involved, which we don't actually know, it might have been some man's daughter or sister."

"That had occurred to me. I didn't want to risk offending you again. You would fit into the category of sister. You have me treading on eggs, Miss Talbot. I had forgotten how thin an English lady's skin can be—and how pretty," he added, stopping to gaze at my cheeks. "Like rose petals." He reached out one finger and touched my cheek gently. "A blushing rose." I felt the heat flush to my face and immediately suggested we continue on our way.

"Must we, just when things were getting interesting?"

"You promised to behave, Mr. Renshaw," I reminded him.

"So I did and so I shall, ma'am, or you'll think me no better than I should be. Shall we blame it, like all my other lapses, on India?"

"You've lost that excuse, sir. You told me the Indians were excessively polite."

As we returned to the curricle, Renshaw said, "You mentioned the name Fanshawe. I heard a rumor that Mr. Stoddart left a book at the inn bearing the name Harold Fanshawe."

"Where did you hear that? I heard nothing of it!"

"One of the ladies you were kind enough to introduce me to mentioned it. Her name was Carter, I believe. You were speaking to that pretty blond lady at the time. Miss Lemon, I think the name was."

Minnie Carter was a reliable gossip. Her upstairs maid had a cousin who served ale at the Boar's Head.

"Do you think he was using an alias, that he wasn't Mr. Stoddart but Mr. Fanshawe?" I asked. I noticed, but didn't mention, that Renshaw had found the time to assess Addie's charms in the few moments we had spent with her.

"It was an old book. It might have been in the family for some time, perhaps belonging to his grandfather or an uncle. Does Mrs. Murray have a large family?"

"I don't know. In the three years I've known her, I've seldom heard her mention her family, except that she has a sister married to a solicitor in Norwich. Oh, and I remember she once mentioned a brother in London, but his name is Henry. I've never seen him."

"You could mention the name Harold Fanshawe to her."

"I've already mentioned Mr. Stoddart. She was at Oakbay when Lollie and I returned from the water meadow. She didn't recognize Mr. Stoddart, either by name or description. In fact, I mentioned Mrs. Murray to Stoddart as well and he'd never heard of her, to judge by his lack of interest."

As we were leaving the meadow, we saw a small funeral cortege filing into the graveyard and stopped to look at it. There had been only the one death in the parish recently. The paucity of mourners bespoke the death of a stranger or a person of no importance. There were only the clergyman, the beadle, the sexton, and the innkeeper's son. The last one, I expect, was there because Stoddart had been staying at the Boar's Head. They all looked more impatient to get on with their own lives than sorrowful at the death.

"That must be Mr. Stoddart they're burying," I said. "They didn't waste any time in doing it." I felt a pang for Stoddart, cut down in his prime.

Renshaw removed his hat. I bowed my head, and we waited until the little procession had passed, then stood at the lychgate a moment. Although there were no official mourners, it wasn't a parish burial. Stoddart had a proper coffin and was taken to a burial plot that had already been dug. An unknown corpse without funds would have been buried with less ceremony in paupers' field.

"I wonder who arranged the funeral," Renshaw said.

Isaiah Smogg, the gravedigger's son, stood beside us. I didn't notice him until he spoke. He was a brash, redheaded, freckle-faced lad of twelve or thirteen who didn't hesitate to eavesdrop and even join in a private conversation. If he had been wearing shoes, no doubt he would have joined the mourners. Isaiah is fleet of finger and foot. It is a common spectacle in Chilton Abbas to see him careering down the street clutching some purloined item under his ragged shirt, with one or other of the merchants shouting after him. He will end up in Newgate if he isn't shot first.

"Mr. Maitland done it," he said, and spat between his teeth. "Paid for the service and lot and box and all since Stoddart was done in on his land. A fine gent, Mr. Maitland. He tipped Pa a quid."

"That's Mr. Maitland all over," I said, beaming in approval. In fact, I was astonished at his having even thought of such a thing. It might equally be said that Stoddart had met his end on Oakbay property, but it had never entered our heads to arrange his burial.

"Is Maitland always in such a rush to perform his charitable works?" Renshaw asked me in a quizzing way.

"Pa said it might be best to wait," Isaiah said, "in case Stoddart's folks showed up. But Maitland, he said, 'Not likely, is it? The sooner the man's buried, the sooner forgotten,' and gave Pa a quid."

"Quite right," I said, and took a step onward.

Isaiah turned his bold eyes on Renshaw and said bluntly, "You're the gent staying with Mr. Sommers. I seen your sporting rig in town—with her in it," he added, tossing his tousled head at me. "A dandy rattler and prads, mister."

"Thank you. I don't believe I caught your name."

"Everybody knows me. I'm Isaiah, ain't I? I'm named after the Bible. I'm a profit."

Renshaw held his face perfectly sober and said, "I'm happy to meet you, Isaiah."

"You didn't say who you are."

"I'm Robert Renshaw."

"You're brown as an Injun. How'd ye get so brown? Are you a sojer from Wellington's army?"

"No, I've been in India."

Isaiah turned his eyes to me and gave a cocky laugh. "You don't want to marry this 'un, Miss Talbot. Them Injuns burn their wives."

"We've already discussed that," Renshaw said.

I didn't want to encourage Isaiah's impudence and went on to the curricle. Renshaw remained behind a moment, talking to him.

"You should have given Isaiah a good setdown," I said when Renshaw returned.

"We were just discussing the murder."

"You take a ghoulish interest in all this."

"Not at all. It's merely mental exercise. A little puzzle to keep the mind active while I'm here. I can't spend all my time chasing ladies. Aren't you curious to hear what I discovered from Isaiah?"

"You shouldn't encourage the boy to gossip. Well, what is it?" I asked brusquely. Of course I was on tenterhooks to hear whatever it was.

"Isaiah is often in the shepherd's hut. He hides there when his papa wants him to help dig a grave. He's seen a couple using it for what he calls 'flings they shouldn't ought to.'"

"What couple?" I demanded at once.

"You're right. I shouldn't encourage gossip. But it was no lady's maid, Miss Talbot. It was a lady and a gent."

"Don't be so provoking!"

"I might tell you . . . if you promise to drive out with me again."

I gave him a saucy smile. "I might drive out with you again . . . if you tell me."

"Might is not good enough."

"You said only that you *might* tell me."

"So I did. I shall now say positively that I will tell you if you'll drive out with me again."

I scowled, feigning displeasure, although I was not averse to going out with him again. "There is nothing to stop me from asking Isaiah myself."

"No, no. It goes against your principles to encourage gossip. Never back down on matters of principle, Miss Talbot. You can save yourself a few pennies by accepting my offer instead."

He helped me into the curricle, joined me, and flicked the whip. "Is it a date tomorrow afternoon?" he asked.

"All right." To remove the triumphant look in his eyes, I added, "You didn't have to resort to bribery, Mr. Renshaw. I might have said yes if you had just asked me nicely."

"You know my opinion of 'might.' Now you've definitely committed yourself. Shall we say threeish?"

"Are you sure Beau won't have other plans? You're his guest, after all."

"Why, to tell the truth, I believe he wishes me at Jericho. We have little in common after all the years apart. I'm thinking of removing to the Boar's Head."

"But you only came here to visit Beau!"

"True, but now I've promised dances to several ladies at the assembly. It would be ungentlemanly of me to renege."

"Much that would bother you," I scoffed.

"Well, then, if you insist on the whole truth, I've found Beau's neighbors so genial that I can't bear to tear myself away. Hops are but poor entertainment when all's said and done. They'll grow equally well whether I'm there to watch them or not."

"Is it a large hop farm, Mr. Renshaw?"

He smiled knowingly. "Twenty thousand acres. It, and my other interests, give me ten thousand a year. I can't complain."

"Ten thousand a year! Why on earth did you ever bother going to India?"

"That's a bride for another outing," he replied, and wouldn't be budged from his position.

"Men who stand to inherit such a substantial fortune don't usually leave home unless they've fallen into disgrace. I'm not sure your story will be fit for a lady's ears," I said.

"Did I mention I also stand to inherit from an uncle?" he asked blandly.

Really, he was too provoking for words. And too intriguing not to have caught my interest.

Chapter Seven

I was prevented from keeping my appointment with Renshaw the next afternoon by a horrid rain that dragged on all day. As Lollie said, it wasn't enough rain to do the crops any good, but it was too much to let us enjoy the outdoors. Renshaw sent a note canceling the drive. I thought he might come for tea to lighten the tedium of a whole day spent indoors with Beau, but he didn't.

Rainy weather always gives Aunt Talbot a fit of the dismals. Her object of scorn that day was Renshaw.

"Taking you to the water meadow, where murderers lurk," she said, shaking her head. "What was the man thinking of, and you, Amy, to go with him? He might have killed you."

"Surely a murderer works more cunningly than

71

that, Auntie," I replied, making a joke of it. "I shouldn't think he invites his victims out on dates before killing them. That would tend to point the finger at him, would it not?"

"You speak as if the murderer was normal. It's quite possible he's a madman seized by uncontrollable fits of violence, like poor Maggie McGee is taken by those fits of stealing. There's not necessarily any sense in it. Maggie's a spinster, and you know perfectly well she took that horn-handled razor from the everything store. I saw her with my own eyes."

Auntie enjoys a good argument. When she is losing, she resorts to supposition. I had a reply to this latest supposition that the murderer was mad, however.

"The murderer stole Stoddart's five hundred pounds. That doesn't look like irrational behavior."

"We don't know the murderer took the money. It's gone, but who is to say Stoddart had it on him? It's a good deal to carry about in his pocket. He might have bought something with it or paid a debt. Speaking of money, Amy, did you get any notion at all of how Renshaw is fixed financially?"

When I told her about the enormous income from his hop farm, she rallied in his favor for a half hour, but when still the rain continued, she soon changed her tune.

"What is to stop a man from saying he has an income of a hundred thousand a year, when no one knows him?"

"Beau knows him," I pointed out. "He told us about the hop farm."

"He didn't say anything about ten thousand a year. Those bucks hang together like burrs when one of them is after an heiress. Don't forget Mr. Maitland in your scurry after Renshaw. If you course two hares at once, you'll catch neither. Personally, I don't believe a word Beau Sommers says. We'll have a look at this hop farm before committing ourselves. Whoever heard of anyone making such a fortune from hops? Now if it were sheep or cattle . . ."

"Belview Farm supplies hops to dozens of brewers. They must make ten thousand a year," I said.

"Good God! Is it Belview he owns?"

"No! I only mentioned it as an example. One sees their advertisements everywhere."

"My wits are gone begging. Of course it couldn't be Belview. That belongs to Lord Travers. That certainly takes the gilt off the gingerbread. For a moment there I thought you were on to something. Travers would never send his heir off to India."

After a few hours of haranguing, I began to have doubts about Renshaw myself. I didn't tell her about his curiosity regarding the murder, or finding the blue ribbon, or, worst of all, his notion of removing to the Boar's Head. She would never countenance the latter especially. When a gentleman visits a friend, he visits him at his home, not a convenient inn. Maitland, on the other hand, was in high aroma for having buried Stoddart with no fuss and no expense to the rate-payers of the parish.

No one called that evening. The rain continued dripping until we finally retired at eleven o'clock.

We were up early the next morning. It was Lollie's custom to rise at seven, like a good farmer. We were at the breakfast table shortly after eight when he came storming into the room. His eyes were open as wide as barn doors.

"The body's gone!" he exclaimed.

"What do you mean, gone?" Aunt Talbot demanded. She didn't have to ask what body. We knew it was Stoddart he meant.

"It's been dug up from the grave. The grave's empty."

For some reason I thought of Renshaw and his extreme curiosity about the murder. "You'd best report it to McAdam," I said.

"Isaiah tells me it was McAdam who had it dug up. Isaiah was watching the men at the sheep dip."

"It's time the rascal did more than watch," Auntie said. "At thirteen he ought to be working, but then who'd hire him?"

"The exhumation is official, not the work of the resurrection men," Lollie continued. "I went to the graveyard myself. The grave is empty."

"Why was the body dug up?" I asked.

"Isaiah didn't know. He said his father had been hauled out of bed at the crack of dawn and asked to disinter the corpse. It was taken into Chilton Abbas.''

It is not to be imagined that our carriage was tardy in following the corpse to the village. We got the details of the story from Constable Monger, who had left his office and taken to the streets in his eagerness to spread the marvelous tale.

''The fambly was found,'' he announced to his listeners. The audience consisted mainly of ladies, with a few gentlemen who had come with their wives or womenfolk.

''How?'' Mrs. Carter demanded.

''There was a special-delivery letter of inquiry from London yesterday afternoon with the lad's description.''

It struck me that even while Stoddart was being buried, that letter must have been on its way. It did seem a little odd, then, that Maitland had rushed the burial forward.

''How do they know Stoddart is the missing man?'' a gentleman asked.

''His brother came rushing down last night, didn't he?'' was Monger's reply. ''He reckanized a few items that wasn't buried. There was a book found at the inn. . . . That was enough to set up the dig. It's all confirmed now. The brother says it was him, right enough.''

''Was he some kin to the Fanshawes?'' Mrs. Carter asked.

''Nay.'' Monger allowed a dramatic pause before making his announcement. ''He was a lord!" Gasps of astonishment caused Monger to stop a moment and smile benignly at the effect he had achieved. When the gasps had subsided, he continued, "But only a younger son. Lord Harry Heston he was, the youngest son of Lord Dolman." None of us recognized the name, but we knew the importance of a title.

"Where is this Lord Dolman from?" someone asked.

"Sussex."

"What was a lord's lad doing here?" Aunt Talbot asked.

"On a walking tour for the good of his lungs. His walk may have cured his lungs, but it proved unhealthy for the rest of him. Let it be a lesson to us."

On this vague warning Monger swaggered along to the next corner, where more people were gathering. Our group remained behind to discuss the finding, with more questions than answers. Why had he called himself Stoddart? was the main question. He wasn't so famous as a Byron or a Brummell that his name would have caused turmoil.

"It was a mighty slow walking tour," Mrs. Carter said. "He was at that inn for three days and walked no farther than to the water meadow. Most of his time was spent sitting in the tavern drinking ale and talking to the locals. Mind you, he had the blunt right enough. That explains the five hundred. A lord's son, fancy! He paid for more than his share of the rounds, they say. Much good all that sluicing would do his lungs. Trying to loosen a few tongues, do you think?"

"He didn't look that frail, either," Mrs. Davis added. "Not fleshy, but not pale or coughing at all. My husband showed him through the church and the lad never said a word about being a lord. He didn't inquire for any Fanshawe, either. It's not like one of them to be shy about putting himself forward."

"He never called on Lord Hadley," Mrs. Carter averred. "You'd think he would as he's a lord. They're all related, you know, everyone man jack of them."

"What did they do with the body?" someone inquired.

"Took it home to Sussex for a proper burial, I expect. It was well done of Mr. Maitland to bury the lad, but he was a bit previous about it," Mrs. Davis said, looking about for support.

"He meant well, though," Mrs. Carter said firmly.

A shout echoed from the sweet shop, and looking up, I saw Isaiah tearing toward us, with Mr. Strong, the proprietor, hot on his heels. Isaiah was holding his shirt, which is where he stores his purloined goods until he is safely away.

He barged into the middle of our group, ending up at my side. "G'day, Miss Talbot." He grinned. "Where's yer fellow today?"

"What are you up to, Isaiah?" my aunt demanded, getting hold of him by the elbow.

"Nuthin'! I ain't done nuthin'."

Mr. Strong was upon us. He hauled Isaiah out by the shirttails and searched him, but he found nothing.

"I saw you taking those peppermint sticks. Where did you drop them, eh?" Strong demanded.

"I didn't take nuthin'. Who'd want yer old peppermint sticks?"

Strong left in frustration. I felt a gentle movement at my side, and when I glanced down, I saw Isaiah's dirty little paw sliding from my pocket, holding three peppermint sticks. He had hidden them in my pocket before being searched. Really, that scamp was up to anything. I didn't make a fuss of it. One accepts Isaiah as he is. Some villages have an idiot; we have a thief. But Isaiah is helpful in many ways. He is always eager to run a message or help find a lost child. Besides, he has it hard at home. His mama is simple and his papa drinks. I've seen bruises on Isaiah on more than one occasion. He denies to the last gasp that his papa beats him, but I suspect it is so.

Lollie, who hasn't the stamina for prolonged gossiping, suggested that we go home. Auntie wanted some white thread for a new petticoat she was making, and we went to the drapery shop to buy it and continue gossiping while Lollie went for the carriage. Mrs. Murray was there, all but sobbing. She had lost Fifi, her small, white cobby dog with long, silky hair. A Maltese, she calls it. It is some rare species her doting husband got for her in London. She pulls the hair off its face and ties it with a ribbon. A blue ribbon, now that I think of it. Perhaps Fifi had been playing in the shepherd's hut.

"I only let her out for a little exercise. She's never run away before. She's suspicious of strangers. She would never have followed anyone. I fear she's been kidnapped."

"No one would steal her," my aunt said. "She'd be recognized a mile away. There's not another dog like Fifi in the county."

"I won't tell you what she cost. You wouldn't believe it. I've asked Mulliner to put a notice in the window. I'm offering a five-pound reward," Mrs. Murray said.

Half the ladies in the shop darted out the door to look for Fifi; the other half remained behind to exclaim over such largesse and then to continue discussing Lord Harry.

As Auntie and I came out of the drapery shop some minutes later, we met Maitland. He looked exquisite as usual.

"Oh, Mr. Maitland," my aunt said. "Have you heard the news about Lord Harry Heston?"

"Indeed I have," he said, doffing his hat and bowing. "McAdam called on me late last night to inform me of it. I'm sorry I rushed the funeral ahead. I discussed it with Lord Hadley. He thought the sooner it was done, the sooner it would be forgotten. It is distressing to the ladies in particular. A strange tale, is it not? A walking tour that ended in murder. Our water meadow is hardly a holidayer's paradise, eh, Miss Talbot?" he added to me with a warm smile.

"Amy wouldn't agree with you there, Mr. Maitland," my aunt said, simpering. "Anywhere there is a wild-flower sprouting is paradise to her."

"I know it well." He gave me another smile. "There are some very pretty bluebells in my spinney. You must feel free to sketch them."

"I'm sticking close to home until they catch Lord Harry's murderer," I replied. I doubted his bluebells were any different from those growing at Oakbay. I would have been more pleased with the invitation if he had offered to accompany me.

"I shouldn't think you have any reason to worry, ma'am. I suspect young Lord Harry got himself mixed up in something in London. A duel, perhaps. If he killed his man, he'd have to rusticate. No one would look for him in this quiet place."

"That might account for his being here under an assumed name, but who could have killed him?" I asked.

"The friends or relatives of whoever he killed in the duel, perhaps. They might have followed him and waited their chance. A sad business for Lord Dolman. The more you stir it, the worse it stinks. My game warden mentioned seeing a tall, young gentleman talking to Lord Harry in the graveyard the day before he was killed. I am on my way to mention it to McAdam."

"What did the gentleman look like?" my aunt asked at once.

The description was vague. The man was taller than average. He had been wearing a hat that concealed his hair. All that was certain was that he wasn't a local man and that he was dressed like a gentleman. I mentioned the similar-sounding stranger Addie had reported being seen in town. Maitland had also heard of him but could add nothing to identify the man.

"An unfortunate business all around," he said, shaking his head. "Very unfortunate. I don't hold with dueling."

Auntie commended him for his proper thinking. We soon saw our carriage approaching and took our leave of Maitland.

Aunt Talbot relayed Maitland's idea to Lollie, who doesn't much care for Morris Maitland. It is actually Maitland's steward he has had a few run-ins with over grazing sheep on what Lollie believes is our land, but Lollie holds Maitland responsible. "Very convenient, this tall stranger who has disappeared," he said.

"No doubt Mr. Maitland has figured it out," Aunt Talbot said. "He is a knowing one, and so kind, burying the body even before he knew who it was. A real gentleman. I wonder if Lord Dolman will reimburse him for the funeral. Kind of Mr. Maitland to invite you to sketch in his spinney, Amy."

"He ain't such a saint as you make him," Lollie said. "I'd steer clear of his spinney if I were you,

Amy. You know his reputation with the ladies. They do say he even fools around with his own servants. When a man fouls his own home paddock . . ."

"I don't believe a word of it," Aunt Talbot scoffed. But she never encouraged me to go to his spinney after that afternoon.

"It's true," Lollie insisted. "I've seen him in the shepherd's hut with that pretty little upstairs maid of his. Sally something."

"Sally Semple is no better than she should be," my aunt said at once.

"No, and neither is Maitland."

After we got home, I mentioned to Lollie that Renshaw had found a blue ribbon in the shepherd's hut.

"There you are, then," he said. "You stay away from Maitland, Amy. He ain't interested in marriage."

"I'm hardly a servant. He wouldn't do that sort of thing with a lady."

"Would he not? He does it with Mrs. Murray."

I gasped in amazement. "Not in the shepherd's hut, surely!"

But once I had considered the matter, I found it was mainly the location that stuck in my craw. The rest was not too difficult to believe. It was common gossip that Maitland was a bit of a rake and it was not completely a secret that Mrs. Murray was no better than she should be, though she usually confined her carrying on to London. But to think of that highly polished pair carrying on in an old sod hut really stretched the imagination. The announcement certainly dimmed the glow of Morris Maitland.

"Why not? It's a nice private place. I've seen her riding in Maitland's meadow before now. When the water is down, I mean. Perhaps he invited her to look at his bluebells," Lollie said with a sardonic grin. "But it's usually his own servant girls I see him go there with."

"Well, I've never seen him, and I spend a good deal of time in the meadow. Oh, speaking of the meadow, Lollie, could you spare me an hour this afternoon? I'd like to continue my sketch of the monkeyflowers."

"We can go now, if you like. I'll have a look at that shepherd's hut and see if I can't find some trace that Mrs. Murray was there. Then you'll know I speak the truth."

"I shall just slip into an older gown. It won't take me a moment."

Chapter Eight

Within five minutes we were headed to the water meadow. I have always loved the meadow, but somehow I felt almost frightened when Lollie left to examine the shepherd's hut and I was alone. The flowers weren't in prime shape for sketching; their heads drooped with the weight of water from yesterday's rain. A steady light *plop* sounded forlornly as water dripped from leaves into the pond below. My table rock was too damp to sit on comfortably, so I leaned against a tree and was promptly dowsed when a breeze stirred its branches. It made a shambles of my sketching pad as well.

Since work was impossible, I decided to join Lollie at the shepherd's hut. As I circled the water, I saw him coming out of the doorway. His face was paper white, his dark eyes staring. My heart shook with fear.

"Not another body!" I gasped.

He shook his head. "Money," he said in a high, unnatural voice. "Whole bloody bags of it. There must be thousands of pounds in bank notes."

My heart slowed to a dull thud as I ran forward. "Where was it? Mr. Renshaw was in that hut recently. He didn't mention seeing any money."

"It was buried beneath the straw."

Of course I had to see this marvel for myself. Lollie went with me. He had pulled the straw bed aside. Beneath it a hole had been dug and in it sat two canvas bags. They had leather straps and locks that had been sealed. The seals had been pried open. By the dim light from the doorway I saw stacks of new pound notes. Fives and tens. I couldn't even begin to estimate how much money was there in all.

"Those seals look official," Lollie said. "I wager this was stolen from a bank or some such thing."

He took one bag to the doorway. The printing was hard to read, for the canvas was dark, but with careful examination we could make out the words "Property of the British Government."

"Egads! Someone has robbed the government!" Lollie said in a strangled squeak. "We'd best report it at once. You go, Amy. I'll stay here and guard it."

"No, you come with me. You don't even have a gun, Lollie. If the thief comes back after it, he'll kill you."

"I'll wager that is why poor Lord Harry was murdered!" Lollie exclaimed. "Odd that the money's hidden on Maitland's land."

"Come with me," I urged again.

"And let him get clean away with it? I should say not! I'll hide if I hear anyone coming. In fact, if Maitland comes for his stolen blunt, I'll follow him."

"No! Let him go! Just your having seen him will be evidence enough. We've both seen the money. Don't take any foolish chances, Lollie. Not that I think Maitland is the thief!"

"It's on his land." He paused for a moment, then added, "Mind you, I would have thought Maitland was too cagey to hide stolen goods on his own property. Pretty poorly hidden, too."

He glanced southward to where Beau Sommers's land meets ours and Maitland's. Sommers's lot is wide and shallow, it faces a road parallel to the road Oakbay is on and touches both our land and Maitland's at the back end.

"Go on and be quick about it," Lollie said. "Call McAdam, mind, not that idiot, Monger."

I ran like a hare through the meadow, looking over my shoulder a dozen times to make sure I wasn't pursued. My bonnet flew off my head, tethered to my neck by its ribbons. In my haste and confusion I had left my paint box behind again. You will realize my state of perturbation when I tell you I didn't think of it for another hour.

"Not another body!" Cook cried when I went pelting in at the kitchen door.

"No, money!" I said, and stopped to catch my breath before continuing on upstairs.

"What money?" Cook called after me.

"Government money—stolen. In the shepherd's hut," I called back, heading for the stairs.

Aunt Talbot was in the morning room, working on her new petticoat, when I ran in. We had debased her morals to the extent that she was sewing a half-inch of eyelet embroidery around the hem.

"What on earth happened to you, Amy?" She took one look at me and leaped from her chair. "Did someone attack you? Not Renshaw?"

"No, no one," I said, and blurted out my story between gulps for air.

"I'll send John Groom for McAdam," Auntie said when I had finished.

"Tell him to take Sandfly. Lollie won't mind."

Sandfly is Lollie's mount, a goer if ever there was one. The groom would be in Chilton Abbas in ten minutes. Meanwhile I was worried about Lollie being alone in the hut with so much money.

"I'm taking a gun and going back," I said.

"You'll do no such thing. That place isn't safe for a lady. Send George with a gun."

"I'll go with him," I insisted. She didn't try to stop me. In fact, she would have liked to come with us, but having decreed it was no place for a lady, she was too proud to back down.

George got Lollie's shotgun and we headed out the back door at a trot. Cook, Betty, and Inez stared as if they were watching a stage play, then ran out the back door behind us to watch our flight.

"This'll put Inez in another tizzy," George said, smiling complacently. He was sweet on Inez and enjoyed playing the hero in front of her. He brandished the gun menacingly as we went.

The meadow was only a thousand yards behind the house, but it seemed at least a mile that day. When the shepherd's hut came into view across the water, I saw no sign of Lollie and forced myself to run faster. But as we drew closer, I took George's elbow, bringing him to a halt.

"Lollie said he'd hide if anyone came. He must have seen someone coming. We'd best proceed cautiously, George. The thief might be in the hut."

We tiptoed forward, hiding behind bushes and peering at the hut. We waited, but when no one came out, we crouched down and inched closer,

closer. When we got to the end of the bushes, George stood up and aimed the gun.

"Come out with your hands up," he called. "I've got a gun."

I watched the hut with my heart hammering in my throat. Who would come out of the doorway? Would it be my hero, Maitland, revealed as a common thief? Would it be Mr. Renshaw and/or Beau Sommers? Or would it be a stranger? I hoped it would be a stranger, the man Maitland's game warden had seen talking to Lord Harry.

It was no one. No one came out. George went closer, calling as he went. I went along behind him, using his broad back as a cover in case of bullets. When nothing happened, I called, "Lollie! It's only me. Where are you?"

It was George who spotted him. Lollie had been dragged through the doorway of the hut. He lay on his back on the floor, unconscious. My first fear was that he was dead, but when I examined him, I saw that he was still warm and breathing. There was no trace of a knife mark or a bullet wound, no rope around his neck. He didn't even have a welt on his head as far as I could see, or a black eye.

"Someone bashed him, looks like," George said.

We carefully dragged Lollie into the daylight to get a better look at him. George kept the gun raised, looking all around, while I checked the back of Lollie's head. I found a lump the size of a plum. Eventually Lollie opened his eyes and blinked a couple of times.

"Amy?" he said weakly and in a confused tone.

"It's all right, Lollie. We're here. Who hit you?"

"They got the money," he said, and tried to sit up.

"Did you see who—"

He was looking less confused and sat up, rubbing his head. "I didn't see a thing. I was hiding in those bushes," he said, pointing to a stand of wild bushes about ten feet from the hut. "I heard a noise behind the hut. It sounded like a harness jingling. I didn't think I ought to go and check since I was alone and without a gun. I shall carry a gun with me from now on, by jingo. Anyhow, I suddenly heard the bushes move behind me. My head exploded, and the next thing I knew, you and George were here. Good lad, George," he said, smiling weakly at our indispensable footman. "And you, too, Amy. You didn't see anyone?"

"No, not a soul. Whoever did it must have dragged you into the hut, stolen the money, and left on his mount. I wonder if he left the money behind, hidden somewhere."

"A nag could easily have carried those two bags. I fancy the blunt is gone, but we'll have a look."

He struggled to his feet, rubbing the back of his head.

"You stay here with the gun, Lollie. George and I will look for the money," I said.

When Lollie agreed to this arrangement, I knew he must be feeling wretched. George and I examined every square inch of the hut and an area within a few hundred feet of it. The bags weren't buried under the straw or tossed onto the hut's roof; they weren't hidden in the bushes or up in a tree. They were gone. The only thing of any significance that we found were hoof and wheel marks in the wet earth behind the hut. Lollie didn't think the thief would use a gig when a mount would do, but the tracks looked fresh. They had been made since yesterday's rain.

Oh, and there were also some drag marks where Lollie had been pulled from the bushes. I think the thief might at least have carried him. His trousers and the back of his jacket and even his hair confirmed that he'd been dragged. And not even by his shoulders but by his feet.

There was nothing to do but wait for McAdam to come and hear the story. That happened about half an hour later. I was surprised to see that McAdam was accompanied by Mr. Murray.

"Mr. Murray was with me when I received your message," McAdam explained. "As he has some interest in the money in question, he came along."

Murray came forward, right hand extended. He is a big, bearlike, pompous gentleman. Like most politicians he has a prosperous belly, smooth jowls, an insincere smile, and can speak a break-teeth language devised to conceal his meaning when it suits him.

"It is my privilege to congratulate you on behalf of the government. You've just saved the nation fifty thousand pounds, Mr. Talbot," he said, pumping Lollie's hand.

"Well, I haven't," Lollie said. "The money's gone."

Murray's jowls shook in consternation. Lollie told McAdam and Murray the story. McAdam has known our family long enough that he believed Lollie. Murray, a relative stranger in town after only ten years' occasional residence, looked a little suspicious.

"Were you incapacitated before you could get a look at the chaps who overpowered you?" he asked.

"I was hit from behind. I don't have eyes in the back of my head," Lollie said irritably. "How does it come you're involved, Mr. Murray? Were you in charge of the fifty thousand pounds?"

"Certainly not! I'm only incidentally involved in my capacity as representative of the good people of the parish. The item involved—that is to say, the money—was government property being used to defray the expenses of the government in its position as guardian of the safety and welfare of the state."

McAdam translated for us. "The money was on its way to the navy base at Southampton. It was stolen three weeks ago by highwaymen not far from London. The government has been trying to get a line on it."

"It's odd we heard nothing of it," Lollie said.

"The government doesn't advertise such occurrences, Mr. Talbot," Murray informed him. "It only puts ideas into the heads of other villains."

"Aye, and makes it look dashed careless the way you handle our money!" Lollie retorted.

"Every precaution was taken," Murray said. "The government has not yet ascertained, despite the most rigorous investigations, how the highwaymen were apprised of the fact that government property was being transported. Very likely they didn't know but just made a lucky hit. The property was traveling in an unmarked carriage. Every precaution had been taken for its safe delivery," he repeated.

"Two armed guards," McAdam explained.

"The guards would have tipped the scamps off," Lollie said, rolling his eyes at the government's folly. "Little it matters to you fellows at Whitehall. It's the taxpayers' blunt."

"Let me assure you, Mr. Talbot, every possible step is being taken to recover the money. Our investigations had succeeded in tracing the property to this part of the country."

"They had a fellow looking about for it," McAdam said. "Well, you heard about Lord Harry's death."

Murray let his chins hit his chest for a moment

in homage to Lord Harry's passing. "One of our brighter lads," he intoned.

"You mean Lord Harry was a *spy!*" Lollie exclaimed. I could see the light of enthusiasm gleam in his eyes. He had actually met a spy! He couldn't have been more thrilled if he had met the Prince Regent.

"I would hardly call him a spy," Murray said, jowls jiggling. "He was a government agent, legally empowered by His Majesty's government to recover the stolen property. I think I can tell you, without exceeding my authority, that his reports to the Cabinet suggested he was having some success in his quest. His unfortunate demise right here in this meadow, only yards from where you found the government funds, confirms that supposition. Pity he met his end before he turned the money in."

"The thieves likely killed him as he was trying to recover it," Lollie said. "Dumped his body in the pond, as they dumped me in the hut."

"That is possible. However, we must not make rash assumptions. We have no substantiation that Lord Harry's demise was connected with the job he was doing for us. He was carrying a considerable sum on him. Robbery was the motive, according to the report we received. His watch and a ring were also missing, I think?" He looked a question at McAdam.

"Quite right, but that may have been done to make the murder look like a common robbery," McAdam said. "At the time of my report, Mr.

Murray, I had no idea Lord Harry was working for the government. Now that we know that . . . Well, it's pretty clear his murder had to do with the job he was doing for you."

"It is possible, I suppose," Murray admitted, rather reluctantly. "We don't want that notion to get abroad, however, or we'd have difficulty recruiting agents to work for us."

"I'll replace him!" Lollie offered at once, with the eagerness of a puppy. If he had a tail, it would have been wagging.

Murray smiled indulgently at that. "That's very generous of you, Mr. Talbot. Your offer does you credit, but our agents are specially trained for their work."

"But a stranger sent in from London wouldn't know our neighborhood," Lollie pointed out. "I've lived here all my life. Why, I already have half a dozen ideas where the blunt might be hidden."

"No offense, Mr. Talbot, but there are bound to be questions raised at Whitehall as to whether you . . . Well, I mean to say—you were alone with the money when it disappeared. Naturally, we, who know you so intimately, don't believe you're involved, but to those who haven't the advantage of your acquaintance . . ."

"Damme, I was knocked stone-cold out. You can see where I was dragged into the hut. Look at the back of my jacket." He turned his back to show Murray the mud. "How could I have taken the money, if that's what you're suggesting?"

"Certainly not, my good man. I'm not suggesting anything of the sort, but those fellows at Whitehall who don't know your character might jibe at appointing you to the position. You see my difficulty in accepting your generous offer."

"That's gratitude for you!" I exclaimed, angry on Lollie's behalf. "My brother might have been killed, and you dare to imply that he is a thief."

"My dear Miss Talbot, I think I made it perfectly clear that I think nothing of the sort." Murray turned his oily smile to Lollie. "Next time you go after thieves, lad, I suggest you take a gun," he said, and laughing, he turned and walked away, murmuring something about writing a report to Whitehall.

McAdam just shook his head and went capering after him, leaving Lollie, myself, and George behind, fuming in rage.

"The nerve of that oiler!" I said, outraged.

"Shh, sis, he'll hear you."

"I don't care if he does."

"It's pretty clear that my reputation is in ruins," Lollie said with a touch of melodrama. This dramatic utterance was issued to pave the way for his next speech. "I shall just have to find the blunt myself and clear my name."

"Let the gentlemen from Whitehall recover their own property. I'm taking you home to put a cold compress on that lump on your head."

I could see his head was aching. He refused the compress but agreed to take a headache powder before turning into an unofficial agent for the government.

We discussed possible suspects. Lollie favored Maitland. I favored the tall stranger Maitland's game warden had seen talking with Lord Harry in the water meadow.

"He's disappeared—if he ever was here," Lollie pointed out.

"Of course he was here. Maitland's game warden—"

"I wonder how much Maitland paid him to see this mysterious stranger."

I liked Lollie better before he became an agent.

Chapter Nine

A note from Renshaw arrived shortly after I reached home. He suggested that as we had missed our drive yesterday, he would call for me that afternoon at three, unless he heard otherwise from me in the interim.

Aunt Talbot went into a rant. She thought it presumptuous of him to assume he could "call whenever it suits him, and you will be sitting on your thumbs, waiting for him. He's only after your money, my girl. If he had a hop farm making ten thousand a year, people would have heard of him. A son with that sort of inheritance waiting for him doesn't go shabbing off to be baked to leather in the sun of India. If I were you, I'd write a note telling him I was busy."

"Yesterday's outing was postponed because of the rain. Surely that is what a postponement means, that the outing will take place later," I said.

"Auntie is right, of course," Lollie said, "but I wish you will let Renshaw come all the same." Lollie had adopted a cynical air to go with his new position as self-appointed agent for His Majesty's government. This air consisted mainly of keeping his eyes half closed, cocking his head to one side, and looking at us mere mortals with tolerant amusement.

He continued, "It must have occurred to you, Amy, that Renshaw arrived hot on the heels of Lord Harry. He might very well be mixed up in this. The shepherd's hut is as handy to Sommers's place as it is to Maitland's."

"Handier!" Aunt Talbot said at once, although it wasn't true. The hut is about equidistant from Oakbay, Maitland's place, and Beau's. "And what is the matter with your neck, Lollie? Do you have a crick in it?"

The neck straightened infinitesimally.

"Actually, Mr. Renshaw didn't arrive until the morning after Lord Harry's death," I reminded them. "We cannot lay both charges against the poor man. If he has stolen fifty thousand from the government, he hardly has need of my dowry." I spoke lightly, making a joke of it, but it was entirely possible that Auntie was right about his being after my dowry. Why should an extremely wealthy, handsome gentleman who could have his pick of the heiresses have his head turned by a provincial miss such as I? He would be in London during the Season selecting an Incomparable for himself.

"Where was he the night before Lord Harry was killed?" Aunt Talbot asked. "I always thought it odd, his arriving so early in the morning from Kent. You remember I mentioned it at the time. He might have arrived the day before and been lurking about the water meadow, looking for Lord Harry."

"Precisely, and I don't leave Sommers out of it, either," Lollie said, peering at us from his hooded eyes. "They might be in it together. Find out what Beau is doing this afternoon, Amy. If he's out, then you occupy Renshaw while I have a look about Sommers's land. I doubt Beau would take the stolen property into his own house. Pretty hard to make any claim of innocence if the government property is found on his premises. Inside the house, I mean. You'd be doing the country a good deed by lending assistance."

"It's money, Lollie. Not some vague property," I said. "You're beginning to sound as pompous as Murray. And if you want to search Beau's land, I'll go with you."

"I'll take George and my pistol," he said. "Invite Renshaw in for a glass of wine before you leave. I'd like a chance to find out what he knows.

Discreetly, of course. He'll never know he's being quizzed."

It was all done just as Lollie wished. I think Lollie overestimated the danger to his reputation, but Chilton Abbas is a hotbed of gossip and there might be a few raised eyebrows at the money disappearing while he was guarding it.

When Renshaw arrived at three, I invited him in for a glass of wine. He had already heard about the incident in the meadow and inquired about Lollie's condition.

"A mere tap on the head," Lollie said cavalierly, but couldn't resist adding, "It left a lump the size of an onion." Then he narrowed his brown eyes to slits and asked cunningly, "How did you come to hear of it, Renshaw?"

"I was in Chilton Abbas this morning. The whole village is abuzz with it. I half expected to see you in bed with a sawbones hovering at your side."

"It would take more than a knock on the head to put me out of commission. You were in Chilton Abbas, you say? What time would that be?"

"Around eleven, I think. Why do you ask?"

I knew the reason. The attack had occurred around ten. I believe Renshaw also suspected the reason for the question, as he went on to outline the rest of his perfectly innocent day without prompting.

"Before that Beau and I were visiting his aunt,

Mrs. McLaughlin, who lives on the other side of the village."

Beau stood to inherit his childless aunt's small fortune and thus dances attendance on her.

"How is Mrs. McLaughlin?" Aunt Talbot inquired.

"She's nursing a bad case of arthritis."

"It's the rain that brings it on, poor soul," Auntie said.

"Beau and I lunched at the inn," Renshaw continued. "I sent that note to you from the inn, Miss Talbot, as soon as I felt the weather had settled down. I was sorry to miss our drive yesterday." He turned to Lollie and added, "I fancy you won't be up to testing my grays for a day or two, Talbot?"

"Damme, there's nothing wrong with my hands and arms. I could drive them today . . ." He recalled what more important business he had to accomplish that afternoon. "Well, perhaps tomorrow," he added reluctantly.

"Shall we set a time?" Renshaw asked at once. "How does the morning suit you?"

"By Jove! As early as you like." In his eagerness Lollie forgot to narrow his eyes. But he soon remembered. "What is Beau up to this afternoon?" he asked.

"He mentioned coursing hares with a friend."

"At Beauvert or at his friend's place?"

"At Beauvert."

That would make it difficult for Lollie to do any hunting for the bags of money. I soon deduced that he meant to keep an eye on Beau all the same.

"I shall take my fishing rod down to the stream," he said. The stream, the same one that floods the meadow in the spring, meanders to and fro through the meadow. Pretending to fish would give him the opportunity to watch Beau and his friend. "My head is up to that much strain."

"Take your gun and keep an eye out for trouble," Auntie said.

Lollie gave her a dampening glance for revealing his strategy.

"I should think the thief is long gone by now," Renshaw said. "He's got the money. He's taken care of Lord Harry. What is there to keep him in the neighborhood?"

"You don't think he's a local lad, then?" Auntie asked.

"You suspect Maitland because the money was in his hut?" Renshaw was so foolish as to inquire.

"Certainly not! Maitland's place is not the only estate near the hut," she replied, and began a fierce attack on her petticoat with her needle. She had the garment carefully arranged to conceal its intimate use. She would never sew a petticoat in front of a gentleman if he could see what she was making.

"True, Oakbay is just as close," Renshaw replied with a glinting smile, "but I'm sure everyone acquits you all of complicity."

"Why would we report it if we were the thieves?" I demanded, high on my dignity.

"That certainly gives you an . . . air of innocence," he said, not exactly stressing the "air" but hesitating a moment before saying it. His meaning was perfectly clear in any case.

Before anyone took issue with this ill-bred piece of impertinence, he changed the subject. "You heard, I expect, that Lord Harry was an agent looking for the money?"

"I thought it was supposed to be a secret!" Lollie scowled.

"It is the greatest secret in the village. Everyone is whispering it behind raised fingers. Some are saying the five hundred that was stolen was payment to whoever tipped him off about where the money was hidden. One percent is not much inducement, but if the finder is honest, it is enough. And if he is not, then no amount would be sufficient."

I looked a question to see if His Majesty's agent had any further questions. Lollie nodded a curt dismissal and I went out with Renshaw.

"Finding the money must have been quite a shock for you, Miss Talbot," Renshaw said, when we were clipping along in his curricle. We were headed in the direction of Chilton Abbas.

"The bigger shock was seeing Lollie knocked unconscious. And that horrid Murray, hinting that Lollie had taken the money and hidden it!"

"You'll be happy to know that no one in the village suspects him. Your brother, I think, is not

102

quite so kind to his neighbors. I can assure you, Beau had nothing to do with it. I was with him the whole time."

"We don't particularly suspect Beau." Nor did I think Renshaw made a totally reliable alibi. They could even be in it together.

"Of course one must consider Maitland," he said. "No one seems to know where he spent his morning. He wasn't in the village."

"He's a busy man. I'm sure he'll have some explanation."

"He's bound to have an alibi—especially if he's the guilty party," he said with a glance to see how I reacted.

I wouldn't satisfy him by flaring up in Maitland's defense. I asked nonchalantly, "You didn't see any sign of the money bags when you were in the hut the day we drove out there?"

"No, nor later that day when I returned for a closer examination. The money was put there after seven o'clock that evening."

"You went back to look?"

"I was just curious to see if the girl returned looking for her blue ribbon," he said, smiling in a way that suggested he might have been joking. "She didn't, but while I was waiting I moved the hay about. There were no bags hidden there at that time."

I refused to tease him about the girl. "Can't we speak of something else? Lollie has spoken of nothing but this robbery ever since it happened."

"I'm sorry to have ruined his afternoon by

telling him Beau is coursing hares. He intended to scout Beau's land for the money, I take it?"

I feigned astonishment. "In his condition? You must be joking!"

"What is this peculiar 'condition' whose only symptoms appear to be a narrowing of the eyes and a rash of leading questions? I diagnose the onset of spyitis."

"Well, I expect he might have a look about while he's fishing. My brother is eighteen years old, Mr. Renshaw. Still young enough to enjoy a bit of role playing. As all the neighbors are under a cloud, you and Beau cannot expect to escape entirely. You, especially, being a stranger in the neighborhood."

"Lord Harry was also a stranger, an innocent stranger. As the Bible says, 'Be not forgetful to entertain strangers: for thereby some have entertained angels unawares.'"

"And some have entertained less celestial beings, no doubt. If you haven't a set of wings to flee danger, I suggest you be careful or you may find a dagger in your chest one of these nights," I warned.

"It is kind of you to worry about me, ma'am."

Our conversation was conducted in a facetious manner. When Renshaw spoke again, he spoke more seriously.

"It wasn't a dagger, by the by. It was a hunting knife."

"Did they find the knife?"

"Yes, quite near where you were sketching,

actually. It had been tossed into the water. It was a common knife with a bone handle, the kind that can be bought anywhere."

"Where did you hear all this?"

"You ought to have gone into Chilton Abbas. That is where one gets all the latest *on-dits*. I kept a sharp eye out for you. I'm happy to inform you that no one suspects you of wielding the knife. The underrated Monger found it. He spent a deal of time examining the scene of the crime. I discovered something else as well."

"And what is that?"

"But you don't want to discuss the case. We shall speak of other things." He looked about and said, "It's turned out a fine day after all."

Chapter Ten

"Mr. Renshaw! What did you discover?" I demanded.

"Still harping on the case? Well, if you insist. Mr. Mulliner doesn't sell, and never has sold, blue ribbons of the type I found in the hut the day before yesterday. 'No market for such dear items hereabouts,' he tells me."

"Is that all? Good gracious, that's not news. Now if you told me the ribbon couldn't be had in Windsor or Woking or Farnborough, you would have something. Not many of us make it all the way to London, but we do get as far as a nearby city from time to time.''

''I haven't had time to ascertain whether Windsor, Woking, or Farnborough carry such a ribbon. And even if I did, there is always the possibility that the ribbon was sent as a gift from even farther away. No, the ribbon, I fear, is a purple herring.''

''Surely you mean a red herring?''

''And you call yourself an artist! Red and blue make purple, *n'est-ce pas?*'' I frowned at this freakish speech. ''Oh, never mind, it's only a joke.''

We did, finally, speak of other things than the murder and the missing money. I asked Renshaw about India and he told me tales of heat and holy cows and monsoons and loll shrub, which is only red wine with a fancy name, of which a great deal is consumed in India. I had heard more interesting tales from Uncle Hillary. I suspected that Renshaw's career had been too raffish to retail any of his stories to a lady. I never did discover why he went. He weaseled out of a real explanation and talked about his love of travel and adventure.

''Very amusing, Mr. Renshaw, but you have not forgotten the price to be paid for my driving out with you?''

''Miss Talbot, I'm shocked!'' he exclaimed with laughter lurking in the depths of his dark eyes. ''Society has a word for ladies who charge for their company!''

"And no doubt you're familiar with it. Never mind that, weasel. You were going to tell me who Isaiah saw in the shepherd's hut."

"I shall require all my attention to come out of *this* unscathed," he said, and drew the curricle to the side of the road near a weeping willow.

"You forgot the best part of Isaiah's tale, ma'am. Doing 'fings they shouldn't ought to,'" he said, smiling. "Do you know, I've been wrestling with my conscience. I shouldn't have struck that bargain with you. It was ungentlemanly in the extreme. I'm surprised you didn't point it out to me at the time, as you are always looking out for my behavior. The female in the case was a lady, and a gentleman never carries tales detrimental to a lady's fragile reputation."

"It was indeed improper of you to strike such a bargain. It can only be my love of gossip that blinded me to its impropriety or I would have called you to account. But once a gentleman has made a deal, he pays the price. Surely that is the very essence of being a gentleman?"

Renshaw drew off his York tan gloves and flexed his shapely fingers. I wouldn't have called his hand a fire hand. His fingers were quite long enough for aesthetic admiration. The emerald twinkled on his smallest finger.

"Paying one's debts is only one of the essential ingredients of gentlemanhood," he said. Then he flung the gloves aside. "Making a jackass of himself to gain a pretty lady's company is another. It was rash, ill-bred, and foolish of me to strike

107

that bargain. I am on the horns of a dilemma here, Miss Talbot. Demmed uncomfortable place to be. Can't you help me out of this appalling position?"

"Never mind trying to shift the onus on to me. So you're going back on our bargain!"

"Not at all. You were kind enough to accompany me and I must pay the price, but can't we reach a compromise? Ask me anything else. Anything. A fair exchange is no robbery." He gazed for a moment into my eyes. I read a challenge there. "Is there nothing of a more personal nature you care to know about me?" he asked in an insinuating manner.

"And you promise to tell the truth?"

He looked leery. "Oh, dear, why do I have the feeling I'm hopping from the frying pan into the fire?"

He was right about that. I meant to give him a good roasting about chasing after my fortune.

"That will teach you to renege on a bargain. I want the truth, the whole truth—"

"And nothing but the truth. You would make a fine lawyer, ma'am. Do you remember Portia? 'The quality of mercy is not strain'd.' More is expected of a lady lawyer than a mere male."

"Flattery will get you nowhere, Mr. Renshaw. My question is: Why are you *really* here? Beau never mentioned you before. You can't be bosom bows. A brief visit to a school chum might pass muster, but you've been with him for days now and show no intention of leaving."

"You make me sound like a piker! I brought him a case of very fine sherry from—" He came to a guilty stop.

"Wine would certainly be the way to Beau's heart. You're not eighteen years old, like Lollie, to be loitering in the neighborhood because of the murder and theft. Are you sure you don't have an ulterior motive for all these drives out with me?"

I sat back, enjoying his discomfort. Auntie had half convinced me that he was courting me for my dowry, and as he squirmed and turned pink, I felt she had hit it on the head. It was a disappointment, but I hadn't quite fallen in love with Renshaw yet. Maitland still had a strong-enough grip on my imagination to prevent it. Blame it on my soft heart—or on Renshaw's boyish embarrassment or on Portia. I let him off the hook.

"It's all right, Mr. Renshaw," I said. "It was obvious from the beginning that you cared nothing for hops. I couldn't quite believe the ten thousand a year, either. You should have made it a more reasonable five. I expect Beau put you up to it. I can almost hear him."

Renshaw sat with his head bent and his ears pink, looking well and thoroughly ashamed of himself. I decided the kindest thing was to make a joke of it.

"My neighbor has fifteen thousand," I said, trying to imitate Beau's deep voice. "Not a beauty, but she ain't an antidote, either, and getting on. She's two and twenty—at her last prayers for a husband. She can sit a mount well enough. Draws weeds for a pastime. Deuced odd gel.''

Renshaw finally lifted his head. "And has blue eyes," he added. His own eyes were alight with laughter, and some lingering embarrassment. "You're too clever for me. I'm sorry, Miss Talbot, but I don't want to leave you with the notion that I'm only a fortune hunter. I *was* left the hop farm. It used to bring in ten thousand a year, once upon a time, and could again with good management.''

"Then why don't you go home and manage it?''

"You're eager to be rid of me! I'm not finished my explanation, ma'am. It wasn't quite the way you say. I merely inquired of Beau if there were any pretty ladies in the neighborhood. He mentioned one or two. 'My neighbor, Amy Talbot, is a pretty chick,' he said. 'I'll introduce you.' 'What does she look like?' I asked. 'She's pretty,' he said again. *I* would have said beautiful. 'Blonde, brunette, or redhead?' I asked. 'Sort of brownish,' he said, 'with blue eyes.' Your bonnet shaded your eyes that morning. I could see they were large and lustrous, but not their color.''

He inclined his head closer to mine, gazing deeply into my eyes. "I've never seen eyes just that shade—lighter than emeralds, darker than peridots. Ripening emeralds, perhaps, before they achieve their full hue.''

There was some hypnotic force in his gaze or in the soft murmur of his voice. As he spoke, his head kept coming closer to mine until our lips were only inches apart. And still he kept up that soft murmur.

"I love the way your hair wantons in the breeze, like a Botticelli grace. Don't look at me like that, Miss Talbot. Is it *my* fault you're so irresistible?"

When our lips finally met, his were still murmuring against mine, which had the peculiar effect of making me feel as if he were nibbling my lips. His speech died on a whisper as he drew me into his arms and his moving lips finally firmed in a real kiss. I had often imagined being kissed . . . by Morris Maitland.

As the embrace deepened, I forgot all about Maitland and gave myself up to this new sensation. In my imagination the kisses had not been like this. They were a localized affair, affecting only the lips. Now I felt a glowing heat gathering inside me and an expanding of the lungs that left me both limp and yet energized. I felt a pulse pounding in my throat. The rustling of the trees seemed to be coming from far away.

I knew I should stop Renshaw, yet I felt powerless to do it. While he kissed me, I just sat like a perfect statue, drinking in all these strange, but pleasant, sensations. My arms made a jerking motion, wanting to hold him, but I managed to control them.

When Renshaw finally lifted his head, I noticed my hands had attached themselves to his shoulders. I gazed at him, wild-eyed with astonishment. My breaths came in shallow pants. Not Renshaw's.

"Control yourself, Miss Talbot," he said. The sparkle of laughter lurked in his eyes as he drew back a curl that had worked loose and tucked it back into my bonnet. His fingers brushed lower to cup my jaw in his warm fingers. "I shall have to insist that you wear green glasses the next time we drive out or the neighbors will think me no better than I should be, letting myself be mauled so intimately on a public road."

He seemed to expect some bantering reply to this. I could think of nothing to say except "I believe we should go home now, Mr. Renshaw," and even that came out in a breathless rush.

"You're not angry with me?" he asked, drawing his gloves back on.

"No," I said witlessly. Then finally normal thought returned to my numbed senses and I added with a wretched attempt at playfulness, "As you said, it's not your fault that I'm so irresistible."

But I knew better, of course. It wasn't Amy Talbot who was irresistible. It was Renshaw, with his nibbling kisses and laughing dark eyes. I looked up and down the road to make sure no one had seen us.

"We're quite alone," he said. "The tree protects us from that house on the hill."

"You certainly keep your wits about you when you're seducing a lady!"

"*Seducing!*" he exclaimed in what looked like genuine shock. "I must take issue with your language, Miss Talbot. Oh, damme, let me call you Amy. How can I give you a proper Bear Garden jaw when I must call you Miss?"

"You certainly may not call me Amy!"

"When we're alone, at least, and don't try to change the subject. I'm not trying to seduce you. Seduction implies some wrongdoing, leading a lady astray from the path of virtue. My intentions are honorable. I'm courting you, not trying to seduce you."

"Why would you bother with me if you're who you say you are?"

He just frowned, as if brooding over the question, while he studied me closely. "I had nothing to say about it. I met you and you were the one. *C'est tout.* I felt as if I had been looking for you forever. It was like meeting the other half of myself." He sounded as if he himself was surprised at his explanation.

I sniffed. He picked up the whip and peered down at me. "*Could* I seduce you, Amy?" he asked. "I'm not saying *may* I—naturally you must feign horror at the notion—but could I? You could have me for the taking. Have you felt nothing of what I feel? Would it be physically possible to seduce you?"

"Not without that whip," I replied sternly, but, in fact, I felt weak in every joint at what he had said. The whole discussion was delightfully improper. He implied that I had some extraordinary power over him. The power of love. It was an awesome feeling. Before it went quite to my head, I said, "I suggest you put the whip to better use and get these horses moving. In fact, turn around and take me home."

His features adopted a more normal expression. "You plan to join Lollie in the meadow, looking for clues?"

"I have some work to do on my sketching," I lied. I would go straight up to my bedroom and lie down on my bed and think about that kiss and Renshaw's announcement that he was courting me. And about whether he meant it or was only joking. He sounded as if he meant it. This being the case, I had to decide whether I wanted him to do so. My body knew the answer, but I must let my mind have something to say about it.

He turned the rig around and cracked the whip over the grays' heads. The curricle moved off at a spanking pace toward home.

"You're not involved with Maitland, are you?" he asked. It wasn't a casual question. A frown appeared between his eyes.

"I've never driven out with him. We're casual friends, no more."

"You say that in a rueful way. And you have a certain . . . tremor in your speech when you speak of him. Makes me jealous as a green cow," he added, grinning.

"He's very handsome," I allowed.

"I'm said to have a good profile." He lifted his chin, showing me his silhouette in profile.

It was indeed a beguiling one: a prominent nose, a strong chin, nice lips . . .

Oh, dear, how complicated life was. Surely a lady couldn't be in love with two gentlemen at the same time. This must be thrashed out in the privacy of my room. I turned my mind to less evanescent matters. I wondered who the lady could be who had been with Maitland in the hut. Really, there wasn't a single soul in the parish I could think of who would do anything so dashing. Except Mrs. Murray! I thought about this, among other things, while we drove home.

When we reached the house, I said two words, "Mrs. Murray," and watched him closely.

His shocked expression told me I was right. "How did you . . . I'm not confirming it!"

"There's nobody else it *could* be. When were they together?"

He just shook his head. "Does it matter? You see why I asked you if you were involved with Maitland."

I now knew Lollie was right about having seen her and Maitland in the hut. It certainly dimmed Maitland's glow. I had always known he was rakish; it had added a certain *je ne sais quoi* to his allure. But to be involved with a married neighbor was different. And a foolish, vain lady besides.

Mrs. Murray was not the sort of woman to cause a man to lose his head or his heart. A great, tragic love affair might have lessened the degradation of it all, but she was merely pretty and available. It would be a convenient dalliance while the Murrays were at home, and when they returned to London, she would be forgotten. I despised Maitland for it, and Mrs. Murray, too.

"She has club thumbs," I said foolishly. What caused it was an image of her hands on Maitland's shoulders, drawing him into an embrace.

Renshaw smiled. "I noticed."

I felt my body stiffen. "When did you meet her?"

If Renshaw hadn't turned pink, I might have thought little of it. He had been in the neighborhood for a few days now. He might have met her anywhere. I might even have believed his answer. But that telltale flush revealed too much.

"Beau introduced me the day I arrived, after we left your place. We met the Murrays in town, just outside the Boar's Head."

"Odd she wasn't wearing gloves on the street," I said, giving him a knowing look. She always wears gloves whenever possible, to hide those ugly thumbs.

"Yes, it's odd," he replied woodenly.

"Thank you for the drive, Mr. Renshaw."

"You're welcome, Amy. Will you be here tomorrow when I call on Lollie?"

"I shouldn't think so. And I would prefer it if you would call me Miss Talbot."

He just shook his head. "You surely don't think I am carrying on with Mrs. Murray?" he asked.

"What is it to me if you are, Mr. Renshaw?"

"*Amy!*" he said in such a familiar, chiding tone. "Don't be like that."

"I'm a little particular about my friends. Folks gossip so in the country. Good day, Mr. Renshaw."

I leaped down without his help and darted to the door. My ankle gave a sharp wince as I ran along, for the curricle seat was high off the ground and I hadn't bothered with the step. I wanted only to dart up to my room, but my aunt came into the hallway when she heard the door open.

"Oh, it's you, Amy. You're back early. I thought you were Lollie. He hasn't come back yet."

"Is George with him?"

"Yes, he should be safe enough. Don't forget we're dining with the Murrays tonight," she said, and turned to walk away.

"You didn't tell me that!"

"She invited us the day I read her palm. In the commotion of the murder and all, I must have forgotten."

The Murrays do a deal of socializing when they're in the riding, to keep the voters in curl. Mrs. Murray was the last person I wanted to see that night, but the appointment had been made and it was one my aunt would have been looking forward to with much pleasure.

It made a diversion and it kept me from harping too much on Renshaw's pretending to be in love with me and his familiarity with Mrs. Murray's club thumbs.

Lollie returned unharmed but in a disgruntled mood. There was no sign of His Majesty's agent but plenty of the fretful boy.

"I couldn't discover a thing," he said. "Beau had three or four of his friends flying all over the meadow, coursing hares. They were at it for hours. I'll go out again tonight after the party at the Murrays'."

"Wait until the morning and I'll go with you," I said.

"You forget Renshaw is letting me try his grays in the morning," he said, brightening.

I had nothing so pleasurable to look forward to. Maitland and Renshaw were both carrying on with Mrs. Murray. I must sit at her table and smile for two hours, listening to Murray pontificate on political matters.

If I had had the slightest inkling how events would turn out, I would have claimed a sick headache and gone to bed. But I didn't know, so I put on my best mint green *peau de soie* gown with the lace insets at the bodice and went forth, all unknowing, to a perfectly hideous party.

Chapter Eleven

It was a ghastly party. The Murrays, with more money than taste, decided to show the provincials the proper way to entertain. The table looked like a silver-shop display, with a half-dozen epergnes parading down the center and silver candlesticks crowding the dishes off the board. The food served looked like works of art and tasted rather like paint and canvas as well. The meat was as dry as leather and the rancid butter sauce tasted quite like linseed oil.

I could see Auntie frowning in confusion at a dish of shrimp arranged in the shape of a whole shrimp, with ruffles of parsley sticking out on the tail end like lace on a gown. Olives provided buttons along the front of the gown.

"It looks so pretty I hate to disarrange it," my aunt said when it was passed to her.

The fowl wore not only lacy anklets of shaved paper but waistcoats of ham and buttons of capers. Another fowl dish had the creature's feathers reassembled and stuck into its tail piece. I personally would have enjoyed the ham more without the boiled pig's head sitting on the same plate. As to arranging little cauliflower teeth around the beef tongue! But enough.

I would probably have found it amusing were it not for the fact that both Maitland and Renshaw sat at the table, one on either side of the hostess, vying for her fickle attention. It was no surprise that Maitland was there; he was a neighbor after all. But how the deuce had Renshaw got himself invited? He hadn't glided in on Beau's coattails, either. Beau wasn't there.

I was seated halfway down the board. Mrs. Murray, with no real social graces, gave me my own brother for a partner on my right side and Mr. Lazenby, a retired solicitor, on my left. The only other young lady there was my friend, Addie Lemon. Her partners were Mr. Davis, the vicar, and her uncle. She and Lollie were usually placed side by side.

When Mrs. Murray rose at the dinner's end to lead the ladies to the saloon while the gentlemen enjoyed their port, she said playfully to her husband, "Don't keep the gentlemen too long, Archie."

Then she waved a kiss in the general direction of her two partners and we followed her out. I had refrained from looking at Renshaw during dinner—one of the epergnes had impeded my vision in any case—but I couldn't control my eyes as we left. He was looking at me in a most guilty fashion. His ears were bright pink.

"Some hostess!" Addie scolded as we left. "Keeping both the young gentlemen for herself. I wonder she didn't have Lollie sitting on her lap." Did I mention Addie has a *tendre* for my brother? I am all in favor of the match, in a few years, when Lollie has matured. "But the dinner was fine, was it not?" she added.

Mrs. Murray received numerous compliments on her cook's ingenuity.

"I brought my French chef, Pierre, down from London with me," she said. "A man handles dinners so much better, don't you think?"

The ladies, every one of whom had a female cook, seconded this idea eagerly. For fifteen minutes Mrs. Murray was kept in good humor by compliments on her dinner and gown. The gown was a splendid affair of sequined gauze over a silk petticoat, very décolleté. Pale blue, to match her eyes and the ribbons in her hair. (Not the same shade as the one found in the hut, however.) I wager her gown would have been the fanciest one at any London ball and was much too ornate for the present society.

When the ladies had run out of compliments, Mrs. Murray moved over to Addie and myself. "Mr. Maitland was singing your praises all through dinner, Miss Talbot," she said. "There is an excellent *parti* waiting to be snapped up. He tells me he plans to buy Chalmers's farm, next door to his own place, you know. He'll be the largest landowner around, next to Lord Hadley."

I immediately began to wonder how Maitland could afford to buy Chalmers's place. It was said to be going for fifty thousand pounds. Surely he wasn't so naïve as to be broadcasting at this particular time that he had fifty thousand pounds to spend if he had come by it dishonestly.

Addie asked about Fifi, Mrs. Murray's missing dog.

"That rascal of an Isaiah found her for me. Well, 'found' is one word for it. It wouldn't surprise me much if he lured Fifi away and hid her for a day to increase the reward. I know she smelled of the pigsty when she was brought back, and the Smoggs keep a few pigs out back. He's sharp as a tack, that Isaiah. He'll amount to something one of these days if he isn't thrown into Newgate first." She smiled in approval of his criminal cunning. I bit my tongue on the suggestion that he ought to take up politics.

Mrs. Murray could no longer tolerate the company of ladies. She rang for her butler and said, "Just remind Mr. Murray that the ladies are waiting, Logan."

The ladies were accustomed to waiting not less than an hour for the appearance of their menfolk, often longer. Indeed, this period without the gentlemen talking loudly about horses and politics was most of the ladies' favorite part of the evening. Looks of astonishment were exchanged at having it curtailed so arbitrarily.

The dame certainly had her husband firmly under her club thumb. Within two minutes the tread of footsteps heralded the gentlemen's arrival.

"They wouldn't have had time to finish their cigars," Aunt Talbot said quietly aside to me.

I noticed that neither Maitland nor Renshaw headed straight toward the hostess. Maitland stopped for a word with Lady Anne Travers, Lord Hadley's sister, and Renshaw looked all around then headed toward me.

I felt my face stiffen, yet I was flattered that I could draw him away from Mrs. Murray.

"Miss Talbot," he said, bowing. "May I?"

I was sitting on the sofa with Addie. The idea was that Lollie should occupy the empty seat on her other side. As Renshaw didn't wait for permission, however, he got the place, and Lollie took the chair next to my end of the sofa.

Lollie leaned forward and said, "By the living jingo, did you ever see such a dinner as that, Addie? Amy ought to have done a painting of it."

"Wasn't it lovely!" Addie exclaimed. She also had to lean forward.

After a few more of these awkward exchanges, it was made clear to Renshaw that he had occupied the wrong seat and he switched with Lollie.

"And what did you think of the dinner, Miss Talbot?" he asked.

"The universal opinion is that it was marvelous," I replied discreetly.

"Highly decorative," he said, also discreetly. "I expect you're surprised to see me here."

I stared coolly. "Why should it surprise me that Mrs. Murray invites a friend to dinner, Mr. Renshaw? I am only surprised that Beau wasn't invited as well."

"He was. After he had accepted on both our behalfs, he was called to visit his aunt. She is in worse case than before. He will spend the night with her. Actually, it is Beau who is her friend. I only met her once."

At that moment Mrs. Murray came smiling forward. "Renny, will you do me a teeny favor?" she asked, placing a possessive hand on his shoulder.

He flashed one angry glance at me, then turned smiling to Mrs. Murray. He rose and said, "Certainly, ma'am. It will be my pleasure."

"I want you to suggest to my husband that we . . . you youngsters would like to dance. I invited Mrs. Davis on purpose to play for us. She's quite tolerable on the pianoforte. It's so boring, listening to this endless prattle of politics."

Addie and I exchanged an indignant glance on Mrs. Davis's behalf.

"Perhaps we should see first if the young ladies do wish to dance," Renshaw said with a leery look at us "young ladies."

I looked away.

"Oh, yes! I should like it of all things," Addie said at once.

"Well, in that case, I shall accompany you, Mrs. Murray," Renshaw said. I could see he disliked to put himself forward so far as to make the request on his own.

"Mrs. Murray?" she asked, and laughed. "We are very formal all of a sudden, *Mr.* Renshaw. You always used to call me Marie in London."

Renshaw's expression reminded me of an animal caught in a trap. He forced a weak smile and allowed himself to be led off.

"I didn't know Mr. Renshaw and Mrs. Murray were friends," Addie said.

"Yes, very good friends, I believe," I said. That intimate "always" resounded in my ears.

"If she dances with him, you'll have your chance with Maitland," Addie said, smiling.

Maitland no longer pleased me, but I did, in fact, have my chance with him for the first dance. Mrs. Murray would allow no music but the waltz, despite Mrs. Davis's not being very familiar with the tempo. As a few of the not-so-old couples came along to the ballroom, we could quite easily have made up three squares. When the Olsens and the Carruthers saw there was to be nothing but waltzes, they returned to the saloon. Lollie danced with Addie.

Maitland displayed quite as little interest in me as I then felt in him.

"I'm surprised to see Renshaw remaining so long in the neighborhood" was his first speech.

"Yes, he's visiting his friend, Sommers."

"He don't spend much time with him," he said. Then he gave me a smile that would have sent me into alt a week ago. "It seems you are the attraction, Miss Talbot. I must commend him on his taste."

"I believe Mr. Renshaw has catholic tastes where ladies are concerned," I replied.

His eyes strayed across the floor, where Renshaw and Mrs. Murray were swooping about like a pair of swallows.

"Like that, is it? Marie should watch herself. Chilton Abbas isn't London. She'll come a cropper."

Maitland showed no sign of jealousy. I began to wonder if Renshaw had either invented that story about Marie Murray being in the hut with Maitland or if Isaiah had been mistaken.

"Have you heard any new reports on the mysterious Lord Harry or the money he was after?" was Maitland's next speech.

"It seems McAdam suspects Jim Figgs, the poacher, of complicity."

Maitland emitted a snort of laughter. "I heard that one. They searched Figgs's place and found nothing but a brace of partridges. They have no idea who the thief is, in other words, and are looking about for someone to arrest. Figgs has never stolen more than a rabbit or a partridge in his life."

I noticed he was looking in a suspicious way in Renshaw's direction. "I can think of a likelier person," he said.

He didn't go on to name names and I didn't ask, but it occurred to me that Mrs. Murray might have learned of the shipment of money to the navy from her husband. And if Renshaw had known her in London, as she said, then he might have learned of it from her. Why else had he lied about knowing her before? What possible reason could he have, unless he was guilty?

"How long has Renshaw been back from India?" Maitland asked a little later.

"A little over two weeks."

"That's odd. At dinner Mrs. Murray mentioned waltzing with him at Lady Siberry's ball. That was over three weeks ago."

"Oh." It was all I was capable of saying. My mind was busily scanning the events leading up to Lord Harry's murder. The money, Murray said, had been stolen three weeks ago. Was that why Renshaw claimed to have been in England for only two weeks? He was beginning to look more guilty by the moment.

Yet it was Maitland who was said to be thinking of buying Chalmers's place. I asked him about it.

"I looked it over. I think he's asking a pretty stiff price, but if I can arrange a mortgage, I might buy it."

Mrs. Murray hadn't mentioned a mortgage.

Suddenly the music was over, and Renshaw and Mrs. Murray were coming toward Maitland and myself. I turned to Maitland and began some bantering flirtation.

"Change partners!" Mrs. Murray said gaily, and seized Maitland's arm.

I looked around the room hoping for rescue. Not an eye was turned my way. Without a pause Mrs. Davis began another waltz. Renshaw took my hand and pulled me into his arms.

"Now this is more like it," he said.

I glared. "More like what?" I asked.

"Don't be like that. I've waited too long to get you alone. I couldn't even *see* you all through dinner. You're angry that I interrupted your flirtation with Maitland," he said in a soft voice.

"We were not flirting. It happens we were having a very interesting conversation."

"What is more interesting than flirtation? If that is not why you're glaring like an angry giraffe, my pet, dare I hope you're annoyed that I didn't stand up with you first? I wanted to, but one's hostess has certain priorities."

"I quite understand that Mrs. Murray has a prior claim on you, Mr. Renshaw."

His eyebrows drew together in a scowl. "What nonsense has Maitland been telling you?"

"Oh, it wasn't Mr. Maitland. It was our hostess herself who mentioned your familiarity with her—in London."

"I can explain—"

"I'm not asking for an explanation, Mr. Renshaw. But in the unlikely case that you and I should see each other again, please don't feel it necessary to lie to me. I'm not really that interested in your doings."

"I met her once, at Lady Siberry's ball."

"And once at several other balls, I assume, since you *always* called her Marie."

"I don't remember. One meets so many people in London. Perhaps she's confusing me with someone else."

"And what is confusing *you* about the time of your arrival in England? Lady Siberry's ball was over three weeks ago."

"I said I returned about two weeks ago! It was a few days ago that I told you that. I may have been in England for more than two weeks."

"So it would seem, unless you have a double calling himself by your name. An identical twin, perhaps," I said ironically.

I hadn't noticed he was waltzing me to the side of the room. Until he waltzed me right out the door, I didn't realize what he had in mind.

Once we were in the hallway, he stopped

dancing and released me. He leaned one arm against the wall, barring me from returning to the ballroom. His lips opened in a smile and he said, "You're jealous, Amy. Don't trouble to deny it. I'm delighted. Why else would you be in the boughs at my calling Mrs. Murray by her first name?"

"You flatter yourself, sir. I'm not jealous. I'm disappointed that a man I mistook for a gentleman would lie."

"Disappointment doesn't cause glares and fulminations, my little goose. Disappointment causes rueful looks and shakes of the head, and in extreme cases a wobbling of the lower lip that can be highly attractive. But not so flattering as jealousy. It is jealousy that lends that angry sparkle to a lady's eyes. And why should you be jealous if you don't . . . care for me, at least a little. If we were alone, I could convince you . . ."

He looked up and down the corridor. I knew what he had in mind, and my heart began palpitating in anticipation. He planned to distract me with another of his magic kisses.

I steeled myself against his insidious charm and said in a voice as cold as ice, "It might be wise for you to leave the neighborhood, Mr. Renshaw. Folks are beginning to wonder why you're here, arriving so mysteriously at the time of Lord Harry's death."

"And Mr. Renshaw is wondering why you have turned into an iceberg only because he knew his hostess in London. There's nothing mysterious about my coming here. And I arrived the day after Lord Harry's death, if you recall."

"An odd coincidence. Did you really drive hell-for-leather all night, only to visit a friend you hadn't seen in years? Sure you weren't closer than London? You arrived at seven o'clock in the morning."

"Good Lord! How did you know when I arrived? Chilton Abbas has an extremely efficient spy network."

I ignored it. "And you called at Oakbay before ten. I cannot think you dashed straight off to me after driving all night."

He gave a "Bah!" of disgust, but he didn't offer any explanation. Then he put two shapely fingers under my chin and tilted my head up, forcing me to look at him. "Can't you trust me just a little, Amy?" he asked in a wheedling tone.

Renshaw certainly didn't look like a thief or a murderer. In fact, he looked extremely attractive, with his dark eyes gazing at me and his elegant white cravat standing out in the shadows. His fingers began to move, intimately massaging my chin.

I felt a weakening stab of attraction and twitched my head away. "I'd as soon trust a fox in the chicken coop!" I replied, and flounced away.

Since his arm was barring the way back to the ballroom, I was forced to walk toward the saloon. Renshaw didn't follow me. I didn't look back, not even when he called, "Foxes have to eat, too, you know."

Chapter Twelve

The older guests had begun a card game. I spent the better part of half an hour watching, all the while keeping one eye on the door, wondering if Renshaw would come after me, and devising the clever things I would say if he did. It wasn't Renshaw who eventually showed up but Lollie, and he was wearing his government agent's face: eyes narrowed, lips pursed into an unnatural smirk. He sidled forward, tossing his head toward the door. I left the group and joined him.

"Something's afoot," he said out of the side of his mouth.

"What is it?"

"Murray summoned Renshaw into his study."

"What do you mean, summoned?" I thought perhaps Murray had caught Renshaw and Marie in some compromising situation. I envisaged a duel or at least a degrading bout of fisticuffs.

"I was standing close enough to overhear them. Murray came up behind him and said, 'A word in my study, Mr. Renshaw, if you please.' Renshaw nodded and followed, meek as a lamb."

"Did it have to do with Mrs. Murray?"

"Eh? Of course not. It was nothing to do with

her. She's been throwing herself at Maitland the last half hour. No, it has to do with the missing property, of course. I found out that much at least."

"How?"

"I listened at the door, and it wasn't easy, either, with footmen trotting by carrying trays of drinks. They were talking about the missing property. I heard Murray ripping up at Renshaw, something about coming here masquerading as something or other. I couldn't quite grasp it, but anyhow Murray had a letter from Whitehall about Renshaw. They spoke of Lord Harry and the water meadow. The words 'government property' were repeated more than once. I think Murray was putting it to Renshaw that he's under suspicion."

"He'd hardly do that if he didn't have enough evidence to arrest him." My heart leaped to my throat. "Renshaw hasn't been arrested!"

"No, just warned, I believe."

My heart began to sink back to its normal place. "Why tip him the clue he's suspected?"

"Perhaps he's trying to rattle Renshaw, stir him up so he goes after the blunt. Planning to run, you know, then Murray will arrest him and recover the property. I'll certainly keep a sharp eye on Renshaw when he leaves this party tonight."

"Where are they now?"

"Still at it in Murray's study. Once Renshaw started doing most of the talking, I couldn't hear a word. He pitched his voice low. Murray can be heard in the next county, from speaking on the hustings and in the House."

I knew Renshaw had lied about how long he'd been in England and about knowing Marie Murray. He had displayed a keen interest in Lord Harry and the water meadow. And now this. What else could it mean but that he was guilty?

Being less naïve than Lollie, I even found a reason why Murray didn't just arrest Renshaw on the spot. It must have been from Mrs. Murray that Renshaw discovered the money was being transported. She was never discreet at the best of times, and with a handsome scoundrel flattering her, she'd tell anything except her age. Naturally Murray didn't want to involve his own wife. I thought perhaps he had arranged a deal with Renshaw: Return the money and no charges would be laid, no questions asked.

Of course it was only supposition, but if true, then Renshaw would indeed go after the money that same night. The question was: Would he return it to Murray or try to sneak away with it, perhaps dart back to India? Surely Murray wouldn't let Renshaw out of his sight until he had the money safe.

Lollie and I returned to the ballroom, lingering a moment outside the study door en route. I didn't expect to hear laughter, but Murray was indeed laughing. It was not only the ladies that Renshaw could bring around his thumb. The laughter was drawing closer to the door. Lollie and I walked briskly on to the ballroom and got inside before the study door opened. Lollie strolled on to stand in the corner, spying on the assembly.

When Renshaw returned to the ballroom, he didn't look like a man who had just been chastised. He was smiling when he came toward me.

"Would it compromise us if we had a second dance?" he asked, taking my hand and inclining his head close to mine. "And do we really care? I should adore to be compromised by you. With so few partners the ladies must either dance with the same man more than once or sit out most of the evening." He squeezed my fingers. I wrenched my hand away.

"I don't feel like dancing, thank you," I said coolly.

"I can think of more interesting things we might do, but as we're at a polite party it's the only way I get to hold you in my arms." He watched closely. I glared. "No, you're right. We wouldn't want to freeze all those happy waltzers. We'll sit out instead. Perhaps Murray will build us up a fire before you turn into an ice block. We'll grab a glass of wine and find some nice, secluded corner away from the hurly-burly. We have to talk, Amy—about foxes, and chickens, and April and May."

"And government property," I added, staring to see if he betrayed himself. He looked conscious, but his ears didn't turn pink. His eyes slid to Lollie, who stood in the corner, examining him suspiciously.

"Government property, eh?" he said. "What big ears you have for a small chick. Do you know, I've just lost my appetite for talking. It's only a temporary loss. Hardly a loss at all, really. More an aversion to your chosen topic. *Adieu, ma petite poule.*"

He grabbed my hand and kissed it before I could stop him. Then he bowed, gave one last charming smile, and walked away.

When he asked Mrs. Murray to waltz, he turned and gave me a saucy grin as if to say, "You're not the only chicken in the coop, miss."

I went and joined Lollie. He was on nettles to go home and change into spy clothes. I decided to go with him. We went back to the card parlor and had no trouble convincing Aunt Talbot she was tired. On the short trip home she was full of gossip and regaled us with what all the ladies had said about the party, especially the dinner.

"Mrs. Carruthers was saying Pierre has a better idea how to dress a fowl than to cook it," she said. "Dress it in men's clothing, she meant. Fancy putting a jacket on it. I'm surprised he didn't add a cravat. All its fine raiments didn't prevent it from being as dry as a lime kiln and tough as white leather. And the way Mrs. Murray hauled the men out of the dining room before they had time to light their cheroots! Ah, it's a sad house where the hen crows louder than the cock, and it's Mrs. Murray who rules *that* roost."

I thought of Renshaw, who had called me his little hen. *Ma petite poule*. One would have to crow loudly, indeed, to outcrow him. He was a regular chatterbox.

Lollie confessed that he meant to spy that evening.

"I think it unwise, but counsel is no command," Auntie said, which was her indirect way of giving permission.

Auntie didn't try to keep him on a short rein. She just told him to be careful. As I didn't tell her I meant to accompany him, she neither counseled nor commanded.

Within half an hour of our arrival at Oakbay, we were heading out the back door, suitably attired in old dark clothing and, in my case, comfortable walking shoes.

There followed three of the most uncomfortable hours of my life. A light mist had already been hovering over the countryside when we left the Murrays'. The night was silver and black—silver sky, black everything else. The trees and buildings loomed menacingly around us.

By the time we got to the water meadow, the mist had deepened to a blanket of fog. If you think finding a needle in a haystack is difficult, you should try looking for two bags of money in the countryside on a foggy night. The search had to be done almost by touch, for we could hardly see past the ends of our noses. By the time we had found our way across the meadow of Oakbay to the hedge that separates us from Beauvert, the hem of my skirt was heavy with mud and my feet were sodden. And we hadn't really begun to search yet.

Lollie was in charge of the mission. As the night was so uncomfortable, he decided we should look in the outbuildings of Beauvert to get out of the damp and fog. I stood guard while Lollie sneaked into the stable. The shadow of Beauvert loomed in the distance before me, a geometrical arrangement of squares with a polled turret at either end. There wasn't a single light on in the whole house.

Lollie has an affinity for horses. He managed to keep them quiet while he searched their stalls and the haystack and feed bins and water trough for the money. When he came out, I could see through the mist that his eyes were narrowed.

"Did you find anything?" I asked.

"Not the money, but something significant, I think. Renshaw's grays are in their stalls right enough, so he came home from the party shortly after us." It pleased me to know that he hadn't remained behind, flirting with Mrs. Murray. "Both of their mounts are missing," Lollie added.

"Where can he be?" I asked.

"Beau wouldn't ride to his aunt's place," Lollie replied. Beau wasn't the he I meant, but I didn't say so. I had a sinking feeling that Renshaw was out rounding up the stolen money.

"No, he'd take his carriage," I agreed.

"Well, he didn't. Beau's carriage and carriage horses are in the stable. He didn't go to his aunt's place at all. It looks as if Renshaw and Beau are

137

out on horseback. They'd want horses to carry those bags of money."

"So Beau is in on it as well!" Perhaps the chief instigator, luring Renshaw into crime . . .

"He's Renshaw's cohort, providing a place to wait until things cool down and to hide the blunt," Lollie said.

"They should be easier to spot on horseback at least."

"Aye, we'll go back to the meadow and keep our ears open for the sound of horses. The devil of it is, we'll never keep up with them on foot. I believe I'll go home and get my mount."

"Why don't we just go home and stay?" I suggested. I was cold, wet, and tired. The law hired men to catch criminals. And perhaps I really didn't want to see Renshaw sneaking around with stolen money.

I fully believed he had stolen it. The knowledge sat like a dark and heavy burden on my heart. I survived by convincing myself that the Renshaw I had come to know and care for didn't really exist. He was only playing a role the real Renshaw assumed to con people.

"You run along to bed, Amy," Lollie said in an avuncular way. "I'll handle this."

I tried in vain to dissuade him as we went across the meadow. It was just before we reached the hedgerow separating Beauvert from Oakbay that we heard the muffled sounds of hoofbeats on damp ground and the jingle of metal. They were coming from our own meadow.

We leaped into the hedgerow and watched as a mounted rider came through a break in the hedge, heading for Beauvert. All I noticed was that it was a broad-shouldered man with a curled beaver pulled well forward over his eyes. It could have been Renshaw.

"Beau Sommers," Lollie whispered. We waited a moment to see if anyone was with him, but he was alone. I held my breath, then released a long sigh of relief when Renshaw didn't appear.

"What was he doing on our property?" I asked in a rhetorical way, but Lollie had an answer.

"He wasn't carrying any bags of money. That much was clear. I expect he was taking the shortcut home from the cockfighting barn. We already knew he wasn't visiting his aunt. I thought it a pretty fishy story when I heard it. He only used that as an excuse to miss the Murrays' dull do. That accounts for his carriage being in the stable, but why is the second mount missing? Obviously Renshaw is using it."

The tension was back, tightening my throat and chest. Where was he, indeed, and what was he doing? It was no innocent errand that took a man out on such a night as this.

We continued home. Lollie entered the stable and I headed for the back door, which we had left unlocked for easy entry. My shoes made no sound on the soft earth as I hastened through the shadows to the dark doorway. A potpourri of aromatic scents wafted by as I hastened past the herb garden. The kitchen window glinted eerily in the mist. I was nervous, peering around, listening.

If I had not been paying attention, I wouldn't have heard the softly chiding whispers, the rustle of movement as someone brushed against the lilacs that grow outside the kitchen window. I drew myself against the wall and peered through the fog. It was two people; I could see that much. It looked like a large man and a small one. My heart hammered in my throat as I stood, listening. Their voices were pitched too low for me to recognize or hear any actual words. If they turned around they'd see me and I felt not the slightest doubt that they'd shoot me. However, they were busy arguing and didn't notice me.

As they disappeared into the blackness beyond the house, I overcame the temptation to run inside and lock the door. I had to let Lollie know that someone was close by. I picked up the spade that the gardener usually left at the back door, handy for the home garden, and ran as fast as my legs could carry me to the barn, ready to use the spade if accosted.

Lollie was just coming out, mounted on his bay mare.

"There was someone at our house, two people coming around the corner as I went toward the house!" I told him. "They went that way." I pointed to the left, toward the water meadow.

"Were they on foot?" he asked. "Did you recognize them?"

"They were on foot. It was two men, a big one and a smaller one."

Even as we spoke, we heard the unmistakable whinny of a horse in the distance. "They have horses waiting!" Lollie exclaimed, and was after them.

I waited for fifteen minutes just inside the stable door. We had a mare about to foal and one of the stablehands was there, so I felt safe enough. In a quarter of an hour Lollie was back, scowling in frustration.

"They got away," he said.

"Which way did they go?" If the larger man had been Renshaw, I figured he'd circle back to Beauvert. They had been heading in the opposite direction.

"Toward Maitland's place."

"Maitland's!"

"They rode right past it, but they knew I was after them. It might have been a trick to con me. I lost them in the fog. The bigger man could have been Maitland."

"And Maitland is planning to buy Chalmers's farm!" I exclaimed.

"There was some talk of it after dinner," Lollie said.

I felt such a relief to be able to point the blame away from Renshaw. Maitland had been my hero forever, yet I threw him to the wolves without a qualm, did it happily, if only it could make Renshaw innocent. That was when I admitted to myself that I cared for Renshaw more than was wise. I was eager to snatch at any thread that might make him innocent.

"Maitland don't ride a black nag, though," Lollie said a moment later. "That new bay of his has a white blaze and white stockings on her forelegs. This was a black nag, or dark all over anyhow. Like Beau's mount and Renshaw's. Mind you, Maitland might have muddied up the white markings to prevent the nag being recognized."

"There are plenty of other dark horses in the neighborhood as well. Murray has that black gelding. What was the other nag like, the one the smaller man was riding?"

"It was ahead. I couldn't get a good look at it in the fog. You didn't recognize the intruders?"

"No, but they seemed to be arguing."

I daresay it was the word *intruders* that gave us both the same notion at the same time.

"What were they doing here at Oakbay?" I asked.

Lollie was already dismounting. He slapped his mount's rump and sent it to the stable, where the waiting groom would take care of it. "Let's see if we can find out."

We made a tour of the house, first outside, to ensure that no doors or windows had been forced open. Then we went and checked within, room by room. Nothing had been touched.

"Perhaps they were just taking a shortcut," Lollie said.

"But a shortcut from where? It's no shortcut

to go through Oakbay from the main road and then on to town. In fact, it's longer."

"We'll have a closer look in the morning," he said.

The government agent was tired, cold, wet, and ready for bed. His sister was in the same state, with the added misery of knowing that Renshaw's mount was similar to the one our intruder had been riding and that his mount was not in the stable at Beauvert.

"What I can't figure out is who the little fellow was," Lollie said. Truth to tell, I had forgotten the second man, the smaller one. "He could be Renshaw's valet or groom. He drives that curricle. The ton often have a small groom for their curricles. Tigers, they call them."

"Renshaw always drives his own curricle."

"That's not to say he don't have a tiger. From his jackets and rattler and prads, I'd say he is up to all the rigs."

I made cocoa to warm us, and as soon as it was done, we went up to our beds. It was not until the next morning that we discovered what the intruders had been up to.

Chapter Thirteen

It was Inez who made the discovery. She told George, who told Cook, who told the butler, who brought Inez to us as we were at breakfast. Lentle, the butler, is a wizened man with a few ribbons of hair stretched across his scalp and dreadfully bowed legs that give his walk an awkward gait. He has been with us for sixty of his seventy years, beginning in the home garden and gradually working his way upward to the front door.

"I have bad news, sir," he said to Lollie, who was the official head of the family. "We've been broken in."

Lollie looked almost pleased at this development. "The devil you say! What . . . where . . ."

"The cellar door, sir. The one we never use. Inez noticed it when she was cutting some lilacs for Cook for the kitchen."

Without waiting to hear Inez's story—and I could see by her staring eyes that she was on thorns to tell it—Lollie rose and darted from the room with his breakfast in his throat. Lentle looked uncertainly at us, then said to Inez, "Tell your mistress, Inez," and he turned and waddled after his master.

Inez began her tale to Auntie and myself. "I never would've noticed a thing amiss, for the door was closed, like, and not a sign o' mischief till I stumbled over a stone whilst picking the lilacs and landed with a bang against that door. I felt a sharp sting. Look at this!"

She held out her hand, where a minute dot of blood in what Auntie calls the Venus mount, and the rest of us call the base of the thumb on the palm side, was the only unusual feature.

"That was a splinter, that was. Cook took it out for me. When it stuck into my hand, I looked close at the door, for if it was a rusty nail that got me, I'd have died for sure. That's when I saw it," Inez announced triumphantly.

"Saw what?" Auntie demanded, frothing with impatience at this roundabout way of telling a story.

"The bit o' splintered wood, all fresh and new, there by the lock, the little square of metal that holds on the loop the padlock fits into."

"Yes, I see what you mean," Auntie said.

"As soon as ever I touched that lock, it pulled away from the door. The loop thing had been pried off and set back into place against the door frame with the lock still in it."

I could no longer contain myself. I rose and went after Lollie while Inez continued her tale to an ever-diminishing audience. My brother was still examining the door when I arrived. The padlock was in just the state Inez had described. The metal plate holding the little loop onto the door had been pried off with the padlock still in it. When rammed back into place, one would never guess it had been tampered with.

We couldn't find the tool used to break in. Its absence suggested to the agent that the intruder had brought it with him and taken it away. The cellar door is set back into the ancient stone and painted black. During our investigation in the fog the night before, neither Lollie nor I had noticed the break-in.

He opened the door and I went in behind him, with Lentle following me. The outer door leads to a low cellar under part of the original Tudor house. The root cellar and wine cellar are adjacent to it, under the newer part of the house.

"There's not much they could steal from here," Lollie said, looking around.

The space we stood in is used for storing wood and coal. I examined the woodpile and coal bin. Both were full almost to overflowing. A mountain of coal reached nearly to the ceiling and the woodpile stretched from wall to wall, so I deduced that the man who broke in hadn't been after fuel.

Lollie soon returned to investigate the wine cellar. There, too, all was as it should be. Neat rows of bottles sat in their accustomed racks, gathering a coat of dust. Lentle looked them over closely and assured us they had not been disturbed.

"It must have been a tramp looking for a dry bed out of the fog," Lentle suggested. "I'll have the lock mended. I believe George can handle it." George has many talents. "No need to send to the village for a lock-smith. The lock is still good. A little carpentry is all that's required."

"Yes, you do that, Lentle," Lollie said.

Lentle went off at as brisk a pace as his seventy years and deformed legs allowed. Lollie turned his narrowed eyes on me.

"It was no tramp," he said. "It was those fellows you saw, the ones who rode off toward Chilton Abbas."

"Will you send for Monger? It doesn't look as if they've taken anything."

"I believe I'll report it all the same. Best to have it on record, you know." I doubt Monger kept records, but Lollie was enjoying himself so much, I didn't talk him out of it.

He held his lamp aloft, peering in over the wall of the coal bin. "What is that!" he exclaimed. "Good God, it looks like a body! Hold the lamp for me while I clamber up the coal pile, Amy."

I did as he asked, holding my breath in horror while Lollie scaled the coal mountain, sending a coal slide down to rattle against the three-foot wall. A few lumps of coal fell out onto the floor. Another body, this one in our own house! Who could it be? My first fear that it was Renshaw was soon laid to rest. The outer garments were rough and grayish, not a gentleman's clothing.

"It's the government property!" Lollie called down. His voice, coming from the enclosed coal bin, echoed hollowly in the small space. Even as he spoke, I heard a loud rattle as the coal mountain gave out under him, sending him down in another landslide of coal, clutching a bag of government property in either hand. The same two bags that had been in the shepherd's hut.

Lollie picked himself up from the sea of coal and clambered out of the coal bin. He wore a coat of coal dust from head to toe and a smile from ear to ear.

"They weren't taking anything last night. They were hiding the blunt here!" he exclaimed. "By the living jingo! Never mind Monger. Send George for McAdam at once! What a pair of clunches they were. They needn't have broken the lock. They could have tossed these bags down the coal chute and no one would have been any the wiser. This points to Renshaw right enough," he added. "Maitland knew about the coal chute. Beau as well. All the locals know about it. It was a nine days' wonder when Mama had it put in."

This was true, and I felt the weight back on my heart. Lollie refused to leave the cellar. He stayed there guarding the loot with the coal shovel while I darted inside to send George off for McAdam and of course to tell Aunt Talbot what was afoot. George already had a hammer in his hand to attend to the lock. He really is a wonder.

Auntie turned bone-white and began to fan herself with her serviette. "Well, upon my word!" she said weakly. "What next? Between murderers and thieves and robbers we're not safe in our beds! Every path has a puddle, folks say; this one is more like a pond."

Inez, who was still with her, ran shrieking to

148

the kitchen to warn Cook and Betty. While pandemonium reigned, the doorknocker sounded and Lentle hobbled in to announce, "Mr. and Mrs. Murray, madam."

"I couldn't possibly do a reading this morning. I'm much too upset!" Auntie said.

"Mr. Murray is here as well," Lentle said gently. Mr. Murray did not usually honor us with his august pomposity.

"Oh, in that case, show them into the saloon, Lentle, and offer them wine. Or tea, perhaps, at this hour. Very early for a morning call," she said, glancing at the head-and-shoulders clock on top of the cabinet. It was only nine-thirty.

"Perhaps it has something to do with the theft and murder," I said weakly. Had Murray had Renshaw followed last night and had that person seen him come here? Had he come to retrieve the stolen property from the cellar?

"Glory be to goodness, we mustn't let him know the money is on the premises!" she exclaimed. "Tell Lollie to hide it, Amy. Bury it under the coal pile."

"We've already sent for McAdam."

"Then we shan't mention it to the Murrays," she said.

I don't know what was in her mind. I expect she was so confused, she hardly knew what to think, and she wanted to protect us from any more involvement than necessary. I daresay it would be difficult to prove Lollie hadn't put the blunt there himself.

"Yes, that might be best," I said.

I was confused, too, but it wasn't confusion that led me to agree so readily. Murray knew that Renshaw was involved. McAdam didn't. If we could let McAdam handle the matter, Renshaw might be kept out of it. He didn't deserve such consideration, but I couldn't bear to think of him being led off in manacles. I would tell him the money was discovered and give him the opportunity to escape back to India and, I hoped, to lead a better life in the future.

We straightened our gowns, tidied our hair, and went to the saloon to greet the Murrays. Mrs. Murray had Fifi with her, cradled in her arms as if the dog were a baby. Fifi's hair was held off her face with a bright red ribbon on this occasion. I must say she was a well-behaved pooch. She never uttered a sound all the time she was there, perhaps because Mrs. Murray kept stroking her neck.

"So farouche of us," Mrs. Murray said, "calling at this hour, but we're having a little rout party this evening. Archie has been called back to Whitehall. Something very important to do with an election. Liverpool wants his opinion on the timing of it. We've accepted half a dozen invitations to parties here at home. All will have to be canceled, so we're having a do this evening to say *au revoir* to all our dear friends. Do say you'll come."

"But we had dinner at your house yesterday," my aunt said.

"I know!" Mrs. Murray said, and laughed gaily. "But at election time, you know, a political hostess entertains more than usual."

Murray cleared his throat and began a tedious speech. "You're giving our friends the notion we're only entertaining them for political reasons, Marie," he said chidingly to his wife. "Nothing could be further from the truth. It is only the pleasure of our friends' company we seek. Truth to tell, I would much rather stay at home at this time of year than go galloping off to London."

"Oh, but the Season is in full swing, Archie!" Mrs. Murray pouted.

"You think too much of such things, Marie. I won't always be a Member of Parliament, you must know. A man must look after his estate as well. I'm not at all sure I shall stand at the next election. I am thinking of asking Maitland if he's interested."

As soon as we agreed to attend, they left to invite others to their soiree. They were not long gone before McAdam arrived. I accompanied him to the cellar, hoping to indicate in some subtle manner that he not mention the money to Murray. I had no idea how this might be done. Strangely, McAdam himself suggested it.

"We'll keep this find strictly between ourselves, if you don't mind, Talbot," he said. Of course he conversed with Lollie. I, being a mere lady, was ignored once I had taken him to the cellar.

"Except for Murray, you mean," Lollie said.

"Not even Murray. He might not let it slip,

151

but his good lady . . ." Mrs. Murray's flying tongue was well known to us all.

"Just so you remove the money at once," I said.

McAdam stared at me in amusement. "Remove it? Oh, no, Miss Talbot. That would be most unwise."

His Majesty's agent was smiling cynically and nodding. "Of course, McAdam. Mum's the word."

"I'm sure Auntie is very eager to have the money taken away," I said. "While it's here, we're a target for further break-ins."

"That's exactly the point, Amy," Lollie explained with great condescension. "The thief's hidden the property here, planning to return for it under cover of darkness. McAdam and I will be waiting for him. Catch him red-handed. I take it that's your plan, McAdam?"

"Precisely, Mr. Talbot, but I wouldn't want to involve an innocent citizen. I'll arrange for help."

"Dash it, it's in my house! You can't keep me out of it!" Lollie exclaimed in highest dudgeon.

"Well, if you feel that strongly about it," McAdam said, relenting.

"Demmed right I do!"

"But why did they hide it here?" I asked.

"Because I was searching any likely spot out of doors," Lollie said. "Naturally Renshaw wouldn't want it found inside Sommers's house,where he's staying. I'm assuming Renshaw is your suspect, Mr. McAdam?"

McAdam's eyebrows lifted in surprise, but he confirmed it. Why, then, had he looked surprised? Was he conning Lollie, or was he only surprised that Lollie knew?

"He won't come before dark," McAdam said. "We don't want to draw attention that we've discovered the blunt is here. I'll have my men hidden outside. For the rest, it would be best if you just go about your business as usual."

"I was to test Renshaw's grays this morning," Lollie said.

"Good. Then do it, but don't mention the money."

Lollie was delighted that he didn't have to forgo trying the grays. I expect he also liked the notion of having a chance to quiz the thief. My fear— or was it a hope?—was that he would give the show away.

George was appointed the task of guarding the bags of money in the cellar. McAdam told him not to repair the broken lock. That might tip the thief the clue that we were on to him.

I didn't deign to appear when Renshaw called for Lollie, nor did Auntie. The post had arrived and she was reading her letters. I went into the park to sketch and caught a glimpse of the curricle from behind a spreading elm as they left. Lollie looked as pleased as punch, holding the reins.

Although they were gone for an hour and a half, I was still sketching when they returned.

Time flies when one is at work. I own I felt an inclination to go into the saloon when I saw Renshaw enter the house, but pride kept me where I was. I was more than ready to go in when at last the door opened and Renshaw came out. He was chatting and smiling in a way that told me Lollie had kept his secret.

The curricle was standing at the front door, but Renshaw didn't climb into it. He struck out into the park, looking around. I failed to see who he could be looking for except myself. His words when he found me confirmed it.

"There you are!" he exclaimed, coming forward at an eager gait.

"Were you looking for me, Mr. Renshaw? I am about ready to go in for lunch," I said, gathering up my equipment and trying not to look at him, lest my eyes betray my knowledge.

He glanced at the fleabane I had been drawing and frowned.

"It's the first fleabane I've seen this year. They don't usually open until June, but the spring has been warm," I said, following his gaze to the page.

I noticed then what a wretched job I had done of it. The petals were all wrong. Fleabane has petals so narrow they are almost like hairs. I had made them too broad, more like a Mayweed or a daisy. I had been so distracted that morning that I paid little heed to my sketching. I looked up, wondering if Renshaw had noticed the deterioration in my work. He was looking at me in such a familiar way. His frown had changed to a smile of satisfaction.

"I've been having the same trouble," he said.

"What do you mean?"

"I think you know. A little lack of concentration. If my mind had been on the job at hand, I wouldn't have let Talbot drive so far, so fast. Especially as I'm leaving this afternoon and want my team fresh."

"You're leaving!" I exclaimed. A shaft of sorrow pierced me like an arrow.

"Why, I thought it would please you, Amy. You've urged me to return to my hops more than once."

In a way it did please me. If he left, then he wouldn't be caught retrieving the money. Or was it a trick? Letting on he was leaving . . .

"Yes, I'm afraid I'll be missing the Murrays' party this evening. Duty calls."

"I see." And while we were all at the party, he'd slip to Oakbay and get into the cellar.

"Mr. Maitland shan't have it all his own way, however," he added with another smile. "Beau plans to attend."

"Back from visiting his aunt, is he?"

"He admitted this morning that he didn't go to his aunt's last night at all, but to a cockfight. The Murrays' dos are too tame for him, but I convinced him to go this evening." His eyes studied me closely. "He has instructions to keep an eye on you for me until I can return," he said.

I couldn't quell the lurching of my heart. I

daresay some of my pleasure showed on my face to hear he meant to come back. I tried to keep a calm expression, but I felt my lips part in a smile.

"That's more like it, Amy," he said softly, inching farther behind the elm. "It will soon be over. And when it is . . ." He reached for me and pulled me behind the concealing branches of the tree, where he drew me into his arms. And I let him. Nay, encouraged him. I went willingly.

He crushed me against his strong chest and kissed me. There was no nibbling this time, but a firm, heart-stopping embrace that sent my senses reeling as his lips firmed demandingly on mine. I felt aglow, as if a sun had arisen inside me, illuminating and warning me from within.

There is no describing the indescribable. You have either experienced love or you have not. It felt like love. I had fallen in love with a thief and a murderer. It couldn't be!

I pushed him away. The words came in a strangled gasp. "Oh, Robert! Why did you—"

He drew me back into his arms, smiling curiously. "Are we discussing this embrace or something else?" His periwinkle eyes, fringed with long lashes, gazed into mine. They weren't the eyes of a murderer. I was as sure of that as of my own name. As to the theft, perhaps he meant to return the money.

"I kissed you because I love you. I fell in love with you because . . . because you're you and I am I. And for once Fate got it right, bringing me here at this time."

My happiness was shadowed by the horrid circumstances of "this time." "Don't bother about the money, Robert," I begged. "Just go to London. Go now and don't come back until this is all over, one way or the other."

"You have the schedule reversed, but I will come back for you very soon, Amy. Will you wait for me?"

"I—"

"And pray, don't do anything foolish, my dear. Let me handle this. I must go now. *Au revoir*."

He kissed me again, swiftly, fiercely, then ran back to his curricle, leaving me alone with my mind in a turmoil, pondering his words. If I had the schedule reversed, then did that mean he wouldn't leave for London until this affair was over? But he was leaving today before the party. Or was he?

I gave it up and thought instead of the sweetest words ever spoken. "I love you."

Chapter Fourteen

Lollie was waiting for me when I went into the house.

"About Renshaw," he said. "I think we might be coursing the wrong hare there. I mean to say, just because he's a stranger in town is no reason to assume he's our villain. It might just as easily be Beau or Maitland. Easier. Maitland has definitely put an offer on Chalmers's place. I heard it in town. Where did he suddenly get so much blunt? I'm not saying Renshaw's innocent, but we have no real proof he's guilty."

I was grateful for his change of heart, but I knew the cause of it: that pair of blood grays.

Auntie seemed distracted at lunch. She scarcely spoke but only pushed her food around with her fork while glancing from time to time at a letter by her plate. Lollie carried the burden of conversation. As his talk was all of Renshaw and his grays, I listened with some interest. Renshaw, he said, was a bang-up fiddler, down as a nail and full of pluck. He had promised to keep an eye open at Tattersall's for a team of grays for Lollie when he was ready to set up his curricle.

I expected a tirade from Auntie at this suggestion, but she just said snidely, "I'm sure Mr. Renshaw knows all about horses, but he didn't learn it in India."

"What do you mean?" I demanded at once. It was the way she said it, so snidely.

"I had an answer to my note to Hillary this morning, Amy." She indicated the letter. "You might be interested to know your Mr. Renshaw never worked for the E.I.C. Hillary has never heard of him. He's obviously lying. Renshaw, I mean. I'd like to know where he got that tanned complexion."

I couldn't see my own face, but I doubt if it looked any more unhappy or outraged than Lollie's. I felt betrayed by Renshaw, and I am half ashamed to admit I took it out on Auntie by suggesting a few things might go on at the E.I.C. that her brother didn't know of.

"Not where personnel being sent to India is concerned," she retaliated. "That is his job, to handle the new recruits being sent out to India."

I watched as the government agent's keen mind went to work and came up with an explanation of sorts.

"The Peninsula!" he exclaimed. "By the living jingo, where else could Renshaw have got those tanned cheeks? I always thought he had a military strut. And that scar . . . Why, he probably took a bullet in battle."

Auntie pooh-poohed this notion. "More likely he went to India on his own and got shot for stealing a horse."

"By Jove, I shall dart over to Beauvert this minute before Renshaw leaves and demand an explanation," Lollie said.

Lollie left almost immediately, but when he returned, he said Renshaw had already left. Lollie had spoken to Beau, however, and was wearing an excited face. Lollie decided to go and speak to McAdam, and if *he* didn't know the story, he would ask Murray.

"Murray certainly knows something," he added.

My faith in Renshaw was badly shaken by all this. I didn't think Murray knew anything good of him. Lollie had described their meeting behind closed doors at last night's party as an interrogation. It was best to discover the truth, of course, but it made a shambles of my mind and heart.

Lollie was gone most of the afternoon. When he returned, I had gone abovestairs to dress for dinner and the party and didn't have the opportunity to quiz him in private. We were to dine at home, but I dressed for the rout in a jonquil crepe gown with tiny yellow rosebuds at the bodice and wore matching ones in my hair. All this elegance did nothing to cheer me.

"I don't know what ails the pair of you," Auntie scolded over dinner that evening. "Amy looking as close to a sulky cod as makes no difference, and all over that impostor who claimed to work for John Company. You have a wolf by the ears there, my girl. And you, Lollie, are smirking like a Bath miss, while we sit on a pile of stolen money, waiting for some bloodthirsty murderer to come and steal it out from under us."

"Steps are being taken to safeguard the property," Lollie informed her.

"I wish we weren't going to the Murrays' party this evening," I said, and meant it. Renshaw wouldn't be there. In all probability I'd never see him again. How could he return, when he had been lying to us from the beginning?

"And that's another thing," Auntie continued. She was in a ranting mood. I knew she had been looking forward to the whist party that had been canceled because of Mrs. Murray's do. "That woman has no sense. Who wants to go to the same house two evenings in a row, to eat mutton dressed up like Jack Dandy? What will she serve this evening, I wonder? Chicken in silk stockings? A salmon in a topcoat?"

"Let us not go, Auntie," I urged.

She considered it a moment, then said, "The whist party has been canceled. Everyone will be there. We either go or sit at home staring at the walls."

"I am quite looking forward to it," Lollie said. He had been looking very pleased with himself all through dinner.

Aunt Talbot regarded him suspiciously. "You aren't usually such a gadfly, Lollie. Cockfights and badger baiting are more your style. As your eyes have narrowed to slits, I see you are expecting something exciting to occur. Something to do with those bags of money in the cellar."

"I expect tonight will see the mystery cleared up," he said, and nonchalantly cut a piece of beefsteak into pieces.

Auntie and I were as one in demanding an immediate explanation.

"It's only common sense. What better time to go after the blunt than when we are all out of the house?" he said with a shrug. "I shouldn't be

161

surprised if that's why Murray is having this do. He is likely helping McAdam. By giving the party, he will give the thief the notion no one is home. I fancy the cellar will have company this evening."

"In case it has slipped your notice, we won't be here," I reminded him. "This excitement won't occur at the Murrays' but here at Oakbay."

"But it will be interesting to see who *ain't* at the Murrays'," he said, smirking.

"Rob—Renshaw has gone to London," I said at once. "Just because he isn't there doesn't mean—"

"Dash it, I ain't talking about Renshaw. I know all about him." He assumed an important expression, quite like Mr. Murray just before one of his lectures.

My heart leaped into my throat. "What do you mean, you know all about him?"

"It's secret information."

"You can tell us," Auntie said at once. "We're family."

It was clear to the meanest intelligence that Lollie was eager to share his news. Ere long, he did so.

"As you know, I had a word with Beau," Lollie began. "Once I heard what he had to say, I went along to McAdam. And once McAdam discovered I knew Renshaw was a dashed hero, he broke down and told me the rest." The word *hero* echoed like celestial chimes in my ears.

"Go on," Auntie urged, leaning forward in her eagerness.

"It's as I said. He was in the Peninsula. A colonel. He only told that plumper about being in India to account for his complexion. That little scar on his forehead—he took a bullet in Spain. It scraped his skull, jarred the brain, and set him to raving, but it didn't penetrate the bone. They thought he was for it, sent him home to die. He recovered on the ship and turned his hand to working for the government. An agent, like Lord Harry. I got that much from Beau, but he wouldn't tell me the rest, so I went along to McAdam, letting on I knew more than I did, and found out the whole truth."

My insides were shaking like a blancmange for joy. A hero! Not a murderer, not a thief, but a hero. And he loved me.

"Well, what is the truth?" Auntie demanded eagerly.

Lollie looked all around for lurking spies, leaned forward, lowered his voice, and said, "This isn't to go beyond these walls, you understand. When London didn't get Lord Harry's usual report, they sent Renshaw down to investigate. He knew Beau and used the visit as a pretext for being here without arousing curiosity. Beau's been in on it from day one. It was Renshaw who notified London that Lord Harry had been killed. It was that sketch of yours that identified him, Amy."

"I remember he looked very shocked when he saw it," I said.

"He would, wouldn't he? He made up some

163

tale about looking for some other fellow, I remember, but that is of no account. Lord Harry was on the trail of the stolen money right enough. His last note to London said a Mr. Fanshawe knew its whereabouts. Lord Harry was authorized to give him the five-hundred-pound finder's fee. Those finder's fees bills were marked, by the by, which is why Renshaw was examining that tenner he changed for me in the village. Just as a precaution. He was afraid it might be in circulation already, but it wasn't. At least he didn't find any marked notes. The fifty thousand wasn't marked. Anyhow, McAdam thinks Lord Harry suspected Fanshawe wasn't the man's real name, but he hadn't discovered who he really was despite hanging about the tavern, hoping the man would come in and be revealed by the locals."

"That's why he claimed to be looking for someone called Fanshawe as an excuse to inquire about that name," Auntie said, nodding.

"That's right. He inscribed the name Fanshawe on that book himself to give an excuse to be inquiring for Fanshawes. Perhaps he thought his room at the inn would be examined by the servants when he wasn't in it, or he may have taken the book to the tavern, where he hung about to quiz the locals. When we told him there had never been any Fanshawes here—you remember, Amy, at the graveyard—he was convinced his contact had been lying through his teeth, for he let on he was a local lad. Unfortunately, Lord Harry was killed before he could discover, or at least let London know, who Fanshawe really was."

"It was Maitland he met in the shepherd's hut," Aunt Talbot said reluctantly.

"So it was," Lollie agreed, "but McAdam says Maitland was right here at home when the money was originally stolen from the wagon taking it to the naval base. How would he discover it was on its way? I think Maitland's meeting with Lord Harry was just as he said—an innocent encounter, as ours was, Amy."

"What about Maitland's buying Chalmers's place?" I asked.

"Mortgaged. Lord Hadley has a finger in it. He is offering surety or some such thing."

"Then who does McAdam think—"

"He don't know. That's what we hope to find out tonight."

"Why did Renshaw go to London at this time?" I asked, revealing where my interest in all this lay.

"Perhaps he didn't," Lollie replied mysteriously.

"Then where is he?"

"I fancy he'll be around when we need him. Well, ladies, I believe I shall skip my port this evening and just go below to have a word with George before we leave for the Murray's little do. Mind what I've told you is all secret."

But before leaving he had his lemon tart and custard.

Auntie was never one to lose track of important

165

items. "What about Renshaw's hop farm?" she inquired.

"Belview," Lollie said, and sat back to watch our eyes open wide in amazement.

"Belview!" my aunt exclaimed. I was beyond speech. "But that belongs to Lord Travers."

"Did," Lollie informed us. "The old boy's stuck his fork in the wall. Renshaw is his heir, his nephew, not his son. I daresay he's picked up the title as well. Twenty thousand acres," Lollie said. "But only half of it in hops. He has cattle as well, and of course tenant farms and all that."

Auntie's chin tucked in, her lips pursed, and her eyebrows lifted. She glanced at me. "Do you think the jonquil does you justice, Amy? I always thought you looked best in your mint green."

"I wore it last night."

"So you did. Perhaps you could do something different with your hair—or change those pearls for diamonds."

"He won't be at the Murrays' party," I said. I knew, of course, what these enhancements were in aid of. I think it especially pleased her that Renshaw had cattle as well as hops. She was no friend of ale.

"What, have you decided you like Renshaw, Indian skin and all, Aunt Maude?" Lollie teased.

"A good horse can't be a bad color," Auntie said bluntly. "You have to expect a few thistles with a good harvest. Tan skin is a small price to pay for a tiara. What is his title, exactly?"

"Travers was an earl, they say," Lollie said.

166

Auntie stared at me in stupefaction. "A countess!" she breathed, referring, of course, to my exalted state if I nabbed Renshaw.

After Lollie left, I went upstairs, but I didn't change my gown or my jewelry. I just sat on a chair by the window, looking out at the lilac bushes, remembering past doings with Robert, and wondering how I would look in a tiara. I noticed Isaiah lurking about. He was an inveterate snoop, but there was nothing to give the game away. McAdam's men hadn't arrived yet.

I understood now why Robert had been in London longer than the two weeks he had admitted to. Saying he had just returned from India justified the pretext of looking up old friends. Of course he would meet Marie at parties, and of course she would immediately ask such a handsome buck to call her Marie. He must have been disconcerted to meet her here. I wondered why he hadn't taken her into his confidence and asked her to pretend she didn't know him. Not that her discretion could be relied on.

When it was time to leave for the party, I gathered up my pelisse and went downstairs. The others were waiting for me.

"Is everything under control in the cellar?" I asked Lollie.

"McAdam will have half a dozen militiamen hiding in the bushes after dark. We'll let George up from the cellar then. He must be growing mold from being underground so long. The dastards won't get away this time. I'd give a monkey to be here, but sometimes our duty lies in quieter pastures. I must keep up an appearance of normalcy."

Then he frowned. "Though why it should matter when whoever plans to come for the blunt won't be at the curst party . . . Really, I think McAdam is overdoing the security aspect. I might develop a megrim and leave early. I'll send the rig back for you and Amy, Auntie."

"Whatever you do, be careful," Auntie said.

I had other things on my mind. I thought I might develop a megrim as well. I wanted to be here when the excitement occurred.

No excitement occurred, either at the Murrays' or Oakbay. Everyone (except Robert) was at the party, and everyone (except Lollie, who left at ten) remained until it was over at twelve sharp. The Murrays were leaving for London early in the morning and didn't want to stay up late. I danced with Maitland and Beau Sommers, who had decided to dangle after Addie that evening, perhaps because she was the only other young lady present.

She only encouraged him because she was annoyed with Lollie for leaving so early. Altogether it was a dull do. Murray's chef didn't have time to dress the food up for the party, so the supper served at eleven was no fancier than we might have served at home. The host and hostess seemed distracted. Their minds, I thought, had already preceded them to London.

"I never did get my palm reading this trip, Miss

Talbot," Mrs. Murray said as we were taking our leave. "And I wanted it in particular, too. You mentioned something about my fate line. You don't think we might do it now . . ." She seemed quite perturbed.

Her husband rolled his eyes up toward the ceiling. "You can have your palm read in London, Marie."

"But no one does it as well as Miss Talbot! I could drop by early in the morning if—"

"We leave at eight!" her husband said firmly. "You can't expect Miss Talbot to be up so early."

"The next time you're home, Mrs. Murray," Auntie said. She was flattered at the lady's eagerness.

Lollie had sent the carriage back for us, as promised. As we drove home, Auntie said, "I'm glad Mr. Murray talked her out of that reading. I didn't want to alarm poor Mrs. Murray, but I didn't like the looks of her fate line the last time I did her reading. The fate line is tricky; it seldom runs in a straight line and then one has to work out the timing. Timing is all in the fate line. I fear Mrs. Murray's fate line is warning her of something bad that will occur very soon. She is about thirty-nine, wouldn't you say?"

"I would have thought thirty-five."

"Not with those crow's-feet at the corners of her eyes. If she's only thirty-five, then she has a few years before it happens."

My mind refused to concentrate on such foolishness. "I wonder if it's over yet—at home, I mean, in the cellar."

"We'll soon know."

We knew within twenty minutes that nothing had occurred. No one had come to rescue the banknotes. Lollie came in from his place of concealment in the lilac hedge when he heard the carriage and asked us who had left the party. When we told him no one but himself had left before midnight, he scowled and announced, "It might be any minute now. I had best get back to my post."

Expecting gunshots at any minute, Auntie and I put out all the lamps and crouched in the dark saloon, peering out the window. When there had been no action by one-thirty, Auntie said she was for the feather tick and went up to bed. I remained below another two hours. When I jiggled awake from a doze at three-thirty with a crick in my neck and one foot asleep from sitting on it, I gave up and decided to go to bed as well.

As I was about to leave, Lollie came inside to make coffee for the men outdoors. After having lived at Oakbay all his life, he had no notion where to find anything in the kitchen. I was recruited to make the coffee while he stirred up the embers to hasten the boiling of the water.

While waiting for the water to reach the boil, he said, "I believe I'll just take a nip belowstairs to see that the money is all right."

"It isn't going to get up and walk away by itself," I said, yawning.

He lit a lamp and rattled down the stairs. I heard him poking about in the coal pile. Within seconds a shout pierced the still night air. "It's gone!" he wailed.

I darted down after him. "Impossible! It must have slipped down behind the coal."

"No, dash it, I checked it when I came back from the party and it was right on top of the pile."

I was thankful he had changed into older clothes for standing guard outside because he immediately leaped into the coal bin and began looking for the canvas bags. After a thorough search the upshot of it all was that there wasn't a sign of the money. No one had entered the house, but the money was gone, vanished into thin air.

Chapter Fifteen

"I'd best let the chief know," Lollie said, and darted upstairs with the lamp, leaving me alone in the dark. I lifted my skirts and scampered up behind him.

I assumed "the chief" was McAdam. Imagine my surprise and delight to see Robert come flying into the kitchen, followed by Lollie. And imagine my astonishment to see Robert had his face covered with dirt to match Lollie's coal dust, lending them both the comical air of boys at play.

In the excitement of the moment Robert didn't notice me standing at the stove. I said nothing but just watched him, eager to see my hero in action.

His knitted garment showed his broad chest and shoulders to great advantage. They most assuredly were not the shoulders of a boy. The pistol in his hand left no doubt as to the seriousness of the matter.

"Why is your face smeared like that?" Lollie asked him as they hastened toward the door to the cellar.

"We did it at night in the Peninsula. A white face makes too good a target," Robert explained. "Guerrillas' powder, we call it."

Lollie turned to the stove, perhaps planning to add a few cinders to his face.

"No time for that!" Robert called to him. He turned toward the stove and saw me. "Oh, Amy!" he exclaimed. His lips parted in a distracted sort of smile. I smiled back in the same fondly foolish way.

They hurried on toward the cellar. Lollie grabbed a lamp, handed it to Robert, and followed him below. Robert cast a questioning look over his shoulder as he left, but he didn't say anything else. I was left alone in the kitchen with the memory of that smile.

I lit another lamp, planning to join them, but before I could do so, they were back.

"It's impossible!" Lollie said, his voice high with indignation.

"Since it's happened, let's assume it *is* possible and figure out how it was done," Robert said reasonably.

The coffee was made. I poured us all a cup.

"The men would like some of this," Robert mentioned. "May I, Amy?"

"Certainly. I made it for them. I'll take it out."

"Prepare a tray, I'll call Forten to come and get it," he said in a very military way. Then he remembered that I wasn't one of his men and added, "If you would be so kind."

Lollie said to me, "Forten's watching this side of the house."

Leo Forten was one of the militiamen. His usual occupation was head clerk at the drapery shop. He was a dapper little fellow with kinky red hair and an eye for the ladies.

I made up the tray and Robert called Forten in for it. It was not Forten who came, however, but a man called Edward Frith, a local solicitor.

"Where's Forten?" Robert asked.

"Perhaps he's relieving himself," Frith said, then they all looked at me and blushed. I pretended to be busy with putting cream and sugar on the tray. A lady knows when to be deaf.

I was thanked copiously by both Robert and Frith, then Frith left with the tray. I half feared the "agents" would banish me to my room for safety's sake, so I drank my own coffee standing behind them, near the stove, on the theory that out of sight was out of mind. I listened as they discussed the possibility that one or more of our

173

own servants might be involved. Lollie objected violently to this. So did I, but I let Lollie defend them.

"Lentle's too old; Cook's too fat; Inez and Betty are too ignorant, and anyhow they're girls. As to George! He'd pluck out both eyes and all his teeth before betraying us. Besides, they've all been with us forever. I'd as soon suspect Aunt Maude or Amy," Lollie said.

"The grooms?"

"If you think Alfie Morrison or his son would steal, Renshaw, you're mad. Alfie taught me to ride when I was in short coats."

This was obviously unanswerable. Robert said, with an air of apology, "I didn't really think this was the work of a servant, but we have to cover all possibilities. Very well, then, how did he get in without any of us seeing him? We'll check all the doors and windows. I take it the kitchen door was locked, as I directed?"

"Yes, I came in that way. I had to use my key to get in just now," Lollie said.

"Right, then we'll check the other doors and the windows."

I was assigned the delicate task of checking Cook's room. She sleeps next door to her kitchen. Her window was closed and the blind drawn. To get in by that means the thief would have had to climb over her bed with her in it. We went abovestairs and checked all the doors and windows there. The front door was bolted on the

174

inside; the French doors in the library were also locked. None of the windows was ajar.

I could see Robert's frustration mounting as we went from room to room. "How the hell did he get in?" he exclaimed when the last means of entry had been found innocent. Then he remembered that there was a lady present and in lieu of apologizing he suggested that I retire.

"Don't be ridiculous," I scoffed. "If you can't behave like a gentleman, you may feel free to swear in front of me, Robert. I did have a papa, you know. I've heard worse than an occasional 'hell' or 'damnation' in my life."

"Sorry," he said at last. "But it's enough to make a saint swear. Well, what next? Do we go upstairs and search the bedrooms? I cannot think it likely—" Then he stopped. "No, of course not. We'll check the cellar. What other means of entry is there via the cellar?"

"The only door from the outside is the one we were watching, the one that was used last night," Lollie told him.

I watched as Robert struggled over this. After a moment he said, "I noticed a coal scuttle by the kitchen stove. How is the coal delivered?"

"By the coal chute," Lollie said.

"That would be the metal cap I noticed under the kitchen window?" Lollie nodded. "It's not big enough for a man to get in, surely?"

"I could get through it when I was a young-ster," Lollie said uncertainly.

The coal chute had only been installed four

years ago. Lollie hadn't grown that much. "You might still be able to. I mean a smallish man might," I said.

Without a word Robert snatched up a lamp and headed for the cellar door, with his two acolytes hard on his heels. We clattered down the cellar steps into the older part of the cellar and the coal bin. We didn't even have to go inside the bin. A fresh breeze was noticeable from where we stood. After a moment's looking, a round circle lighter than the wall around it became visible above the tip of the coal mountain. Someone had removed the cap of the coal chute, slithered down the metal shaft to the coal pile, and stolen the money.

"I should have noticed that!" Lollie exclaimed, deeply chagrined. "I did feel a breeze, you know, but in the excitement of finding the money gone, I never gave it another thought."

"That's understandable," Robert said, but his face was stiff with frustration at having to work with such amateurs. "I should have thought of it myself."

"It would take some work to get the money out that way," I said, remembering the size and heft of the bags.

"It couldn't be done," Lollie confirmed. "It's easier to slide down than clamber out. I know, to my sorrow."

"He'd need a good stout rope," Robert said, "but I doubt he took it out that way. He would have put the cap back on the coal chute opening if he had. I fancy he climbed up the cellar stairs and left via the kitchen. I noticed there was no lock on the door leading from the kitchen to the cellar."

"No, there isn't," Lollie said, looking sheepish.

There used to be one, but Lollie had climbed down the coal chute the week it was installed and couldn't get back out. Mama had spent hours looking for him. He had been locked in the cellar. It was a washing day and Cook had been in the wash house, so she hadn't heard him knocking and calling for hours. Mama had had the lock removed then and it had never been replaced.

"Let's confirm our theory," Robert said. "We'll check the stairs and kitchen for signs of coal dust or dirt. But why didn't Leo Forten see him when he left? Perhaps Forten is in on it. What sort of fellow is he?"

"Oh, I shouldn't think he's that sort," Lollie said uncertainly. "Though now that you mention it, he does spend a deal of time at the Boar's Head. Lord Harry might have been keeping an eye on him."

They ran ahead to question Forten. I dallied behind, checking for dirt and coal dust along the way. While they were gone, I spotted several black fingerprints on the wainscoting of the kitchen walls. Cook would not have let her girls leave the kitchen in that state.

Within two minutes the men were back, carrying an inert Leo Forten. Robert held him by the shoulders, Lollie carried his feet. They deposited him on the settle in the corner, where Cook takes her afternoon rest in the winter when she doesn't want to leave her warm kitchen.

I feared the man was dead until Lollie glanced up and said in disgust, "He's drunk as a Dane. We told him not to drink while on duty. It's what comes of using amateurs." His scowl suggested that he had been an agent all of his eighteen years.

With such comments, and taking into account that both he and Robert had their faces and hands smeared with dirt, it was hard to take them seriously. But when Robert spoke, his voice held such authority that I could take him seriously at least. Indeed, I was impressed with his taking charge so effectively. I could well imagine him leading his men into battle in Spain.

"Have a look around for the bottle, Talbot, and let me know if it's from your cellar," he said.

Lollie darted out. Robert turned to me. "Was it a good party, Amy?" he asked.

"No, it was very boring."

He smiled in satisfaction. "It has been my experience that the company makes the party. Dare I hope you feel the same?"

"Why didn't you tell me who you really are?"

"I really am Robert Renshaw."

"I don't mean your name!"

"The one who reports a murder is always considered a suspect," he said, rather playfully. "Then the added coincidence of Lollie's stumbling on to the money and its disappearance . . ."

"You actually thought we were thieves and murderers!"

"Just as you thought I was," he reminded me.

"That's different. You're . . . were . . . a stranger."

"So were you a stranger to me, at first. Later, I was curious to see if you loved me enough to believe in me even when you had some reason to suspect I was dishonest. Call me an egoist or a romantic. Or just call me yours." Then he happened to glance in the little mirror over the sink that Inez had installed when she took up with George and saw his black face.

He smiled at the mirror and turned to me, with his white teeth flashing in his black face. "You really must care to keep a straight face while I prattle of love, looking like this." He looked just fine to me.

Before I could say so, Lollie was back with an empty wine bottle. "This was in the lilac bushes outside the kitchen door. It ain't one of mine," he announced. "The label's been soaked off, but I haven't seen one just like this before. It's paler than most wine bottles."

Robert took the bottle, tilted it into his palm, and tasted the dregs. "Drugged," he said, and examined the bottle carefully. It looked like an ordinary wine bottle to me, perhaps a bit lighter than our own.

"Ask Forten where he got it," I said.

"We shall, as soon as he comes to," Robert replied. He went to the sink, got a glass of water, and poured it over Forten's face. Forten spluttered a moment before settling back into a peaceful snooze.

"We shan't learn anything from him for a few hours," Robert said. "We can't wait that long to get on with the mission. Now let me see. Our thief gave Forten the drugged wine. Forten was guarding this side of the house, which is also the side where the access to the coal chute is. The thief let himself into the cellar via the coal chute, brought up the bags, and left by the back door, setting it to lock behind him."

"He must know Forten can identify him," I said. "It seems he doesn't care if we know who he is."

"That suggests he plans to take off and not return," Robert said. "He could get halfway around the world on fifty thousand pounds. Still, having to leave the area pretty well eliminates any landowners," he added, not entirely happily.

"That lets Beau off the hook," Lollie said to me.

"And Maitland," I added.

Robert smirked. There is no other word for the smug expression that seized his lips. He was happy I had my old favorite, Maitland, in mind for the suspect.

"Whoever he is, he must have made a few trips," Lollie said.

They finally examined the floor, where traces of fresh earth and coal dust were visible, though they didn't stand out on the deep maroon oilcloth floor covering, another of Mama's innovations. I pointed out the finger marks on the wainscoting as well.

Robert reached out to them. I noticed his fingers were a good eight inches higher than the fingerprints on the wall.

"The fellow was bent under the weight of the bags and touched the wall for support," Lollie explained to me.

"Perhaps," Robert said, massaging his jaw with his fingers. When the fingers came away soiled, he remembered his darkened face and drew out a handkerchief to wipe away the dirt. Lollie left his on.

I examined the fingerprints on the wainscoting. They were even lower than where my fingers touched the wall, about an inch lower. They were small, more or less the size of my own. Robert took my hand and placed it over the fingerprints. I felt a rush of warm feeling shoot up my arm at his touch. It was perfectly obvious, however, that Robert's mind was all on business.

"These might almost be a lady's fingerprints," he said.

"The servant girls don't bring up the coal for the stove," Lollie said. "That's George's job, and he's nearly as tall as you. His hands are large."

"Curious," Robert murmured. A frown creased his brow. "There aren't any criminal midgets in the community, I suppose?"

"Only Isaiah," I replied. "Good Lord!"

"What is it?" he exclaimed.

"I saw Isaiah lurking in the yard when I was dressing for the party. You don't suppose that scamp had a hand in this?"

"Where does he live?" Robert asked.

"With his father, in that flint cottage across from the church. The house goes with the job of gravedigger and graveyard maintenance man."

"How would Isaiah know the money was there?"

"He might have seen it being put in the cellar. He's a regular busybody."

"You can't sneeze without Isaiah knowing it— and stealing your handkerchief," Lollie said.

"Isaiah, eh?" Robert said. His eyes narrowed in a way Lollie would approve of. "It's a possibility. We'll look into it, but first we'll try to pick up a trail outside. Does Isaiah have a donkey or a dog cart?"

"He travels on shank's mare," I told him.

"Then he's only a tool at most," Robert said. "Perhaps not even that. I have another idea who might have left those finger marks on the wall." He looked at the fingerprints, then at me, as if measuring the absent villain against my five feet and five inches. "No, don't ask. I shan't malign any of your friends until I have at least an iota of proof."

He massaged his chin again, then said, "Amy, I'm sorry to disturb your household, but would you mind rousing Cook? I want to know what time she retired and if she noticed anything—"

"She was just going to bed when I left the back

182

door to join the militiamen around eleven," Lollie said. "She hadn't noticed anything amiss."

"So the theft occurred between eleven and three-thirty." Robert looked at me. "Did anyone leave the party early, Amy?"

"No, except for Lollie, we all left around midnight. Plenty of time for any of the guests to have done it between twelve and three-thirty, though."

"Only a child, or a woman, could have wiggled down that coal chute," Lollie said.

"And a woman could scarcely have hauled those bags upstairs without making a racket as they thumped from stair to stair," I pointed out.

"Not without help," Robert agreed. "Of course, once she was inside, what was to prevent her from admitting her helper via the back door, since Forten was unconscious?" He went over and examined Forten, who was now snoring stertorously.

"We'll need lanterns, Talbot," Robert said, turning back to us. Lollie flew to obey the chief. "We'll try to pick up the trail from the back door. The mount would have been several hundred yards away to avoid detection. I fancy the bags were hauled to the mount. That took a strong back," he added, frowning. "I wouldn't have thought . . ."

We waited. When he didn't expand on that curious suggestive statement, I said, "Wouldn't have thought what?"

"I think Renshaw means one smallish person

couldn't have done it," Lollie said, rooting out two lanterns from the shelf of the cupboard.

"Exactly," Robert agreed. I didn't think that was what he meant at all. He had already explained that the smaller person could have admitted a helper by the back door. He saw my questioning look and said, "I thought the attempt would occur during the Murrays' party while the family was out of the house."

"But all our suspects were at the party," I said.

Robert nodded, frowning. He sent Lollie for McAdam, who was apprised of the situation and had nothing to add but that he should never have trusted Leo Forten. He was a deal too fond of the bottle, but he had never drunk on the job before. As it was too late to do anything about it, Robert just took a deep breath and said anyone could make a mistake.

McAdam volunteered to remain in charge of the operation at Oakbay while Robert and Lollie tried to pick up the trail outside. No one mentioned where I should be in the meanwhile. I knew well enough that the gentlemen wouldn't allow me to go with them. As nothing was said one way or the other, I flew upstairs, got my oldest pelisse, changed my kid slippers for walking shoes, and sneaked out the front door.

I followed behind Robert and Lollie until they were well beyond the house, at which time I made my presence known. They had either to let me join them or accompany me home. I soon convinced them that speed was of the essence.

And besides, I had brought a poker with me, so I felt perfectly safe.

"That's what we thought about the money." Robert scowled. "Stick close to me. That's an order."

To ensure my compliance, he grasped my hand, the one not holding the poker, and we examined the earth for signs of disturbance. The earth at the back door is clay, packed hard by centuries of footsteps. An elephant could have dragged a house over that clay without leaving much in the way of a mark, so we were unsure which direction to take.

"This is hopeless," I said. "We can't possibly find any traces before morning. I think we should go back to the house and think about this."

"You do that," Robert said at once. "This is no place for a lady."

"What will you do in the meanwhile?"

"Catch the thief," he said complacently.

As he obviously knew a good deal more than he was saying, I decided to remain with His Majesty's agents.

Chapter Sixteen

"Do you know where you're going, Robert?" I ventured to inquire after we had "tracked" through the meadow quite at random for the better part of half an hour. *Tracking* was the word he and Lollie used.

It was much too dark to see any tracks a person might have left in the tall grass. The moon was obscured by a slow-moving patch of clouds and we didn't use the lanterns to avoid being spotted. One or other of the agents would squat from time to time, peer into the grass, and exclaim, "This way!" with great certainty, but invariably the "track" petered out to an untrampled stretch of rank grass.

"Why do we not have Isaiah hauled out of bed and quiz him?" I suggested. "Those were surely his finger marks on the wainscoting. It's exactly the sort of thing he'd do."

"Rob a government caravan of fifty thousand pounds, you mean?" Robert asked ironically. "A bright lad!"

"No, I mean sell his services to whomever did steal the money. He's involved at this stage. He knows something is all I meant."

I might as well not have spoken. "This way!" rang out again, and we were off in the direction of the water meadow. I was convinced the gentlemen hadn't a notion what they were doing but only wanted to be doing something.

"Surely they wouldn't throw the money into the water?" I said. "Unless they were abandoning it . . . But in that case, why bother to remove it from the cellar?"

"Not the water meadow, the shepherd's hut," Lollie deigned to inform me.

"They've already used it once."

"What's to stop them from using it again?"

"The fact that you found it the first time."

We hurried along to the shepherd's hut, where we found things exactly as we had left them some days ago. There was no fresh mound of straw to look under. The place had obviously not been used at all, even for a romantic tryst.

I remembered the blue ribbon Robert had found there and said, "Did you ever discover whether that length of blue ribbon was available in Woking, Windsor, or Farnborough, Robert?"

"Beau checked it out for me. It wasn't available in any of those towns. The drapers think it came from London. Maitland might have bought it for one of his, er, friends."

"So he might. Or your London friend, Mrs. Murray, might have been wearing it. She wears a great many ribbons." Too many, but I didn't say that.

"She also has a pretty parlormaid, Annie. I noticed Annie rolling her eyes at Maitland at the party. I expect Annie gets some of Mrs. Murray's discards."

He was only teasing me that my erstwhile *tendre* was flirting with servants at the shepherd's hut. My mind was going in a different direction. Mrs. Murray was not only a flirt; she also gambled and not for chicken stakes. Might she have fallen into debt in London? When you came down to it, Murray was the only one in the neighborhood who knew for certain that the money was being shipped and his wife might have discovered it from him. Or indeed Murray himself might be involved.

Something was niggling at the back of my mind, but I didn't think it had to do with ribbons. Something else about Mrs. Murray—and Isaiah. Fifi! That was it.

"That rascal of an Isaiah found her for me," Mrs. Murray had said. "Well, 'found' is one word for it. It wouldn't surprise me much if he lured Fifi away and hid her for a day to increase the reward. I know she smelled of the pigsty when she was brought back, and the Smoggs keep a few pigs out back. He's sharp as a tack, that Isaiah. He'll amount to something one of these days if he isn't thrown into Newgate first." She had smiled in approval of his criminal cunning.

She knew he was clever and amenable to criminal activity. He had been loitering about Oakbay last night . . .

While I brooded, Lollie had climbed up on the roof of the shepherd's hut to survey the countryside, either for hiding places or signs of criminal activity. The clouds had moved away from the moon, greatly improving visibility.

I hesitated to mention my suspicions to Robert lest he think me a jealous female, but as the Murrays were leaving in the morning, time was of the essence. I took a deep breath, and after reminding him of Isaiah's presence at Oakbay last night, I told him about Fifi and Mrs. Murray's gambling.

He considered it for a moment, then said, "The ribbon, I think, is an irrelevance involving romance, not robbery."

"I wasn't referring to the ribbon."

"Not directly, but it did occur to me that the lady's carrying on with Maitland might have aroused your ire and caused an unconscious dislike that—"

"Don't be an ass!" I scoffed. "I'm not jealous, if that's what you're implying."

"You did seem mighty fond of Maitland."

"I was also fond of sugarplums and dolls once upon a time. One outgrows those childish fascinations."

"Good," he said with a little smile, and squeezed my fingers. "But about Isaiah, Mrs. Murray is not the only one who realizes he'd sell his soul to Satan for a quid. The whole parish knows it. I have trouble envisaging a lady behind a scheme of this sort. Odd your suspicions don't spread to include Mr. Murray." His quizzical smile suggested that I was jealous of Marie and trying to blacken her character.

I rescued my fingers from his grasp. "I believe a female is quite capable of larceny without a man's help, but in fact it had occurred to me that they might be in it together," I said, refusing to acknowledge his taunt.

"This sudden dart to London when no real crisis exists is interesting. The government has been discussing the election for a month. The

189

cabinet will decide the date. They wouldn't call the members back only for that."

I felt a sense of urgency building. The money had vanished from my brother's house. If it was not found, there would always be a suspicion that we had managed to hide it. I could almost feel the neighbors' eyes squinting at us every time we bought a new gown or had a room painted. "I wonder where the money is coming from?" they would ask in that insinuating way.

"They might have the blunt in their carriage this minute while we waste our time looking for it," I said, to give Robert an idea that we didn't have all night.

"I'll have Isaiah hauled out of bed and quiz him," he said.

"This way!" sounded from the roof of the hut.

"Oh, dear, he's spotted a badger or an owl," I said wearily.

Robert's lips quirked in a grin. "You have a poor opinion of us," he said.

"Only of your tracking instincts. You're not hound dogs, after all."

"What is it?" Robert called up to Lollie.

"Someone just darted through the meadow. He's heading off past the water meadow toward the road."

"Are you sure it isn't a hare?" I asked. "They do forage at night."

"It was bigger than a hare," he said, but he sounded uncertain. If it had been a person, he would have said so.

In any case, he leaped down from the roof and took off, skirting the water meadow. Robert grabbed my hand again and we followed him at a less lively gait, pelting through the long grass, with the wan moon shining above and reflecting in the water. A soft breeze cooled our brows as we hastened along. Lollie let out a loud "Halloo," and "Wait up there!" but the "hare" either didn't hear or didn't heed him.

We followed Lollie up toward the graveyard, where silent marble sentinels made our behavior seem uncouth. We continued on past to the church. When we caught up with him, he was sitting on the lychgate, gasping for breath.

"He got away," he said.

I looked up to the church and Isaiah's house, just across the road. "Isaiah!" I exclaimed. "I knew he was in on it!"

"It could have been him," Lollie said. "It wasn't big enough for a man."

"Let's go to his house now," I said, urging Robert forward with a hand on his elbow.

"I didn't see him go home," Lollie said. "I lost him around the water meadow, but I'm sure it was a person, not a hare or a dog. It was running on two feet."

"We'll see if he's home," I said, again nudging Robert forward.

We all set off for Isaiah's little flint cottage. It looked snug and innocent; no lights were burning within. It seemed rude to go banging on the door at such an hour. I could see Robert was reluctant to do it, but he continued pacing toward the house at a determined gait.

As we crossed the road and were close enough to see details, I noticed some movement at the side of the cottage. Who should it be but Isaiah, strutting forward, fully dressed. That is to say as fully dressed as he ever is, in a ragged shirt, dark trousers that stopped just below his knees, and no shoes.

"Good evening, Miss Talbot," he said, as cocky as ever. But he was breathing rather quickly after his dart through the meadow. "Does your auntie know you're out so late?"

"Mr. Renshaw wants to speak to you, Isaiah, about a most important matter," I said.

He looked at Robert, crossed his arms, lifted his chin in the air, and said, "Fire away, mister."

"I notice you haven't been to bed yet," Robert said in a friendly way designed to put him off his guard. Little did he know Isaiah Smogg.

"Course I have," he said, and yawned theatrically, stretching his arms. "I just got up to check my traps."

"You're not wearing a nightshirt," I said.

"Never do, do I? Don't hold with them. Don't hold with shoes and all that sissy stuff." He spat on the ground to show his disgust of civilization as we know it.

"Oh. What traps are they that you set?" I asked.

"Rat traps," he said with relish. "Ma's got rats in the pantry. They get in through the holes in the floor. Ate half the rabbit she planned to stew for dinner."

He went toward the porch, a rickety affair propped up on rocks, picked up a forked stick, and began poking under the porch. He drew out a trap that did indeed hold a rat as big as a kitten. He held it up by the tail, swinging it under my nose. It was still alive. It squealed in a most disconcerting way. I leaped back but managed to suppress the scream that rose in my throat.

"He ain't quite dead yet," he said. "I'll finish him off in a bucket of water. Cruel to let the poor bugger suffer."

In the meanwhile he set the trapped rat aside and straightened, staring at us mutinously. "You didn't come here to see if I was in bed. What are you after?" he asked.

"The money you took from the cellar at Oakbay," Robert said. He didn't sound angry or questioning but spoke in a normal, everyday sort of voice.

"Don't know what you're talking about," Isaiah replied.

"You were seen, Isaiah," Robert informed him. "Do you know what happens to people who steal from the government? They're hanged."

"Got to prove it first, I reckon. I didn't steal nuthin' and you can't prove I did."

"Where's the money?" Robert asked. "It will go easier for you if you help us."

"I don't know nuthin' about no money. I don't

know what you're talking about. I'm going to bed—soon as I drown this here rat."

On this bold speech he turned, picked up the rat trap, in which the rat was still making agonized squeals, and walked away. I gave Robert a commanding look. He just watched Isaiah go.

"Aren't you going to arrest him? Question him, make him tell what he knows?" I asked.

Lollie looked disappointed in his hero, too. I noticed a frown of disapproval gathering between his eyebrows.

"The lad knows something," he said to Robert. "It was him I followed through the meadow right enough. Didn't you notice he was struggling for breath? We can't just walk away from it."

"Yes, we can," Robert said.

He put his hand on my elbow and led me off. Lollie remained behind a moment, then followed us.

"I'm not questioning your judgment, Renshaw," he said in a very questioning sort of way, "but I do think . . ." He peered back over his shoulder.

I suddenly stopped as a horrible idea occurred to me. "If someone is using Isaiah, Robert— Well, they won't want him around to tell the story. They'll kill him!"

Robert stood perfectly still, frowning. "Isaiah's no amateur. He knows he's involved in serious crime. He was frightened beneath his bluff show. He'll keep his mouth shut to protect himself. He must have demanded a heavy bribe for his part in this." Then he turned to Lollie and asked, "Is he looking at us?"

"Yes, he's come back around to the front of the cottage."

"Good!"

"If he weren't guilty, he wouldn't have bothered watching us," Lollie said.

I was beginning to understand that Robert had a plan. "I think Robert wants Isaiah to think we're leaving, Lollie," I said.

"Ah!" I felt, rather than saw, Lollie's eyes narrow. "We'll go on a ways, then sneak back and watch him," he said.

"Exactly," Robert said. "If Isaiah is as wide awake as I think, he'll follow us to make sure we're going away. We'll continue to that dark patch of road where the elms conceal us, then go back."

"That's halfway home!" Lollie objected. It was more like a quarter of the way.

"Yes, we'll have to move fast once we're out of sight," Robert replied unconcernedly.

We did as Robert said. When we felt the shadows of the elm afforded enough concealment, we stopped and looked behind us. Isaiah was just taking to his heels, heading across the road toward the church.

"That's odd!" Robert exclaimed. "I thought he'd head for Chilton Abbas."

"The Murrays', you mean?" I asked.

"Yes. Where can he be going? Beau's place is across that meadow."

"Good God! You mean he's working for Beau Sommers!" Lollie exclaimed. "And you've been in Beau's pocket all along. He knows every move you've made."

Robert didn't confirm it, but he didn't deny it, either. I was surprised, but I could believe it of Beau. We ran like hares till my throat was dry and my lungs ached. By cutting through the field, we should have been able to see Isaiah as he got to the meadow. But when we had reached a point that showed us the whole scope of the meadow, from behind the church to a flat land of several hundred yards, there wasn't a sign of him. No movement disturbed the rank grass. He hadn't had time to reach the shepherd's hut. The wily scamp had out-smarted us.

"Could he be hiding among the tombstones?" I suggested, as they were the only items large enough to conceal a small boy. The Hadleys' tombstones, in particular, were quite large.

"Either that or he's doubled back and headed to town," Robert said.

We hastened toward the graveyard, keeping a sharp eye out for any untoward movement. At the graveyard we stopped and looked all around.

"I wager he's gone back home," Lollie said, pitching his voice low. "He knew we'd be watching and plans to wait another hour. We'll hide and wait him out, eh, Renshaw?"

Robert replied in a whisper, "You do that. I'm going to take a run into town. On horseback, I'll overtake him if he's outsmarted us and is on his way to the Murrays'. May I borrow your mount, Talbot?"

"Certainly."

We took one last look at the graveyard. The mound of earth that had been removed when Lord Harry was disinterred offered good concealment. I said nothing but just pointed to it.

Without a word Robert darted forward, crouching low to the ground. Accustomed to such exercises in the Peninsula, he went like lightning, his footfalls making no sound on the soft grass.

Lollie and I couldn't keep pace, but we followed behind him. Apparently Isaiah hadn't heard our approach, for when we got to the grave, he was busily stuffing the five- and ten-pound notes into his shirt-front. He wasn't behind the earth mound but in the grave hole, sitting on one of the canvas bags of money with his feet in dirt to the ankles and rapidly emptying the other bag.

When he looked up and saw three faces peering at him, he licked his lips nervously and then grinned. He actually had the sangfroid to grin!

"Look what I found, Mr. Renshaw!" he said. "I do believe it's the money that was stolen, ain't it?"

Robert lifted him out of the hole by his shirt collar. Bills floated from his hands and shirt as he was hoisted up, feet kicking, oaths flying from his lips. Lollie grabbed the money as it flew, to return it to the canvas bags.

"Who are you working for?" Robert asked.

"You're for the gibbet if you don't tell me." He set Isaiah on terra firma but held on to his bony wrist. I had seen Robert's lips quirk in a smile and knew his harshness was a charade to frighten Isaiah.

"You ain't got nothing on me!" the whelp had the gall to say after being caught red-handed. "It ain't agin the law to walk about the graveyard at night. I was following a rabbit."

"How did you plan to catch it? You don't have a gun," Lollie said sternly.

"I didn't plan to catch it. I was trying to find the nest, to take the young 'uns. A dandy stew me ma makes out of a baby rabbit."

"Too late for stories, Isaiah," Robert said.

"Arrest me then. Take me off. See if I care. You're only making a fool o' yourself, mister." He offered his bony wrists for manacles. "Go on. Arrest me! Take me to the roundhouse. I've always wanted to see what it's like."

"I'd rather have your cooperation," Robert said.

"Come on, arrest me," he taunted. "You can leave him to watch the loot." He gave a contemptuous toss of his head toward Lollie.

"Let's talk instead," Robert said, and folded his arms in a patient attitude. The three of us formed a guard around the prisoner. "You can't be too deeply involved. I think you were only used to remove the money from the cellar at Oakbay."

"Was not! I told you, I was just out chasing rabbits when I happened to fall into this hole and found the money. I didn't take none. You can't say I did!"

As he spoke, he fished his hand under his shirt to make sure he had got rid of the last of the bills.

"You were stuffing it in your shirt when we got here," Lollie charged.

"I was only going to take a few samples to McAdam to see if it was the stolen blunt. I should get the five hundred reward."

I heard a muted gasp from Robert at this bold speech. Looking at him, I saw he was having difficulty suppressing an eruption of laughter. "That looks like coal dust on your cheeks," Robert said. This was a bluff. Isaiah's face was so dirty he might have been a guerrilla himself.

"I help Jed Russell deliver coal all the time." This was true—and he would certainly know about our coal chute.

"Shall we go?" Isaiah asked cockily. "I'm ready. What are we waiting for?" He turned and would have walked off to the roundhouse by himself if Robert hadn't grabbed him.

"Your eagerness for the roundhouse surprises me," Robert said blandly. "Why, it's enough to make me think you're eager to get us out of here before your cohorts stop by to pick up the loot. We shall stay, Isaiah."

Isaiah gave him a look that would have melted forged steel, then wrenched himself loose and took off at a fine pace. He ran like the wind, but Robert's legs were longer. He soon had the boy collared and dragged him back.

"Tie him up and gag him, Talbot," Robert said. "We don't want him making a racket when they come for the blunt."

Tying Isaiah up was like trying to tie the wind. He squirmed and wriggled and shouted until Robert stuffed a handkerchief into his mouth. Isaiah promptly spat it out. Renshaw inserted it again and tied it in place with Lollie's handkerchief, to prevent him from shouting to warn his cohorts. Robert, ready for any contingency, had ropes in his pocket with which they bound Isaiah's hands and feet. When the poor boy was trussed up leg and wing like a chicken for the oven, they carried him off to the shadows at the back of the church.

Lollie was left in charge of him. Lollie would have preferred to remain at the grave for the arrest, but his chief insisted rather sternly that he guard Isaiah. By calling the boy "the prisoner" Robert convinced Lollie that his job was vastly important. And so it was. It wouldn't take that little eel long to wiggle free if left unattended.

Chapter Seventeen

Robert and I, he with his pistol cocked and ready, waited behind the shoulders of a large monument to one of the deceased lords of Hadley. The fitful moon chose that moment to disappear behind a

200

ragged drift of cloud. The frisson that shivered up my spine was due to the collection of headstones, each the last visible token of a spent life. Robert used the shiver as an excuse to put his arm around me.

"I shouldn't have let you come," he said.

"I wouldn't have missed it for the world," I replied, snuggling against his warmth.

A light chuckle echoed from his lips. "Aren't you forgetting something, Amy?" Robert asked. "You didn't remind me I had no authority to prevent your coming."

"I took for granted you knew it by now. It was enjoyable, but you know I can't help feeling sorry for Isaiah despite all." I didn't harp on it, lest Robert take it as criticism of his part in it. Naturally a criminal must be punished, and it was myself who had egged him on to accost Isaiah.

"It was the rascal's pluckiness that struck me," Robert replied. "He's still a child but with the nerve of a canal horse. If I can convince him to cooperate, the law will go easy on him because of his age. And that will only turn him loose to continue his immoral way," he said sadly. "Something should be done for him."

To lighten the mood I said, "We haven't had such excitement in the parish as tonight's escapade since Beau's bull got loose one market day and rampaged through Chilton Abbas. It overturned a carriage and three vegetable stalls." An image of a younger Isaiah snatching up dusty cabbages and apples flew through my mind.

201

Robert lifted my chin with one finger and tilted my face up to his. Moonlight reflected in his eyes. We were so close I could feel his breath on my cheek.

"Pretty stiff competition!" he said. "But then I'm not really interested in upsetting carriages and carts. It's only one young lady's heart I hope to wreak havoc on."

The arm holding me tightened, his other arm closed around me, and his lips lowered to mine in a sizzling kiss that warmed me through and through. As his lips burned on mine, something inside me swelled and grew, stirring an indescribable excitement that touched me to the deepest core of my being. I wrapped my arms around him and squeezed tightly. I felt I'd fly off the ground if I didn't hold on to something solid. It was that sort of kiss.

He lifted his head and gazed at me for a long moment, while neither of us said a word, yet I felt a perfect understanding was reached. I was grateful for the cool breeze that fanned my fevered brow. Then he kissed me again long and passionately. When I opened my eyes, I was surprised to see that we were in the graveyard. I had forgotten the rest of the world.

"When this is over, Amy . . ." he said in a husky, intimate tone. He stopped suddenly and shook his head.

"What? What were you going to say?" I asked eagerly.

"No, my wits are gone begging. Whoever heard

of proposing in a graveyard? We shall wait until this is over.''

Well, at least he had used the word *proposing*. We wouldn't have long to wait. A lightening of the sky in the east heralded the approach of dawn. I was still not certain who would come. Beau Sommers was still in the picture. He was always in need of money, and while I had never heard that he was one of Mrs. Murray's flirts, it was possible. Or it might even be a stranger, some London thief. That would be the best of all.

It was no stranger who finally came. They arrived not in a carriage but in a donkey cart. To further confuse the issue, the lady wore trousers and a man's jacket and curled beaver, as she had worn the night she put the money in the cellar of Oakbay. They drove the donkey cart right into the graveyard, up to the side of the grave, at which point the driver, a bulky man, tossed the reins to the lady dressed as a man and hopped out. The driver then lowered himself into the grave and with considerable difficulty hoisted one of the bags out.

''It's been trifled with!'' he exclaimed. I recognized Mr. Murray's voice.

''That demmed Isaiah!'' Marie Murray exclaimed, and climbed down from the donkey cart. She was wearing a footman's outfit and presumably one of her husband's hats. ''Where is he? He was supposed to keep an eye on it!''

''You shouldn't have trusted a boy,'' her husband scolded. ''He's fallen asleep, likely.''

"Not he!"

The second bag was hauled up. We watched as Murray hoisted the bags into the donkey cart, his broad back straining at the job.

When the evidence was in place, Robert whispered, "Now!" and we went quietly forward. Robert's pistol was pointing at them.

"Mr. Murray—and Mrs. Murray," he said grimly, "under authority of His Majesty, I arrest you."

I had never before in my life seen such an anguished expression as I saw on Mr. Murray's face and I hope I never see it again. The strangest thing of all was their total silence. They just looked at each other, Marie frightened to death and Mr. Murray's lips twisted in anguished despair. He took his wife into his arms and pressed her head to his shoulder. She sobbed softly, clinging to him.

After a moment Murray looked up and said in a gruff voice, "We'll go quietly, Renshaw. You can put the pistol away." All his political eloquence had left him and I liked him better for it. "We planned to return the money to the government. We didn't plan to keep it, I promise you. And by the way, I want it on record that I am the one who took it. I am responsible. My wife is innocent."

Robert cast a questioning look at Marie, then said to her husband, "You realize, Mr. Murray, you're admitting to murder as well. Lord Harry—"

"No, no! He was killed by a tramp. His death has nothing to do with this. His watch and purse were missing." He looked a question at his wife, who nodded vigorously.

"There'll be an official investigation, of course," Robert said. "It won't help that you suborned a minor to assist you."

"Isaiah offered!" Marie said at once.

Lollie had been watching and listening from behind the church. When he saw that the criminals had been captured, he joined us, hauling Isaiah along. He had unfastened Isaiah's hands and feet but had tied the lad's wrist to his own with one of the ropes to prevent escape.

Robert turned to Isaiah. "Did you offer your services to the Murrays?" he asked.

Isaiah looked a question at Marie, who glared at him. "Are you still taking me to Lunnon, missus?" he asked her. He looked at Robert's pistol and the defeated air of Mr. Murray.

"What are you talking about?" she scoffed.

"You said you'd take me to Lunnon with you!" he howled. "That's the only reason I dunnit. You said your man would protect me if I was caught. You said they couldn't harm me if I was helping an M.P. You *promised!*"

"Isaiah offered his services," Marie repeated, trying to muster an air of dignity.

"Did not! You ast me." He turned to Robert. "It was all *her* doings." He pointed his free hand at Mrs. Murray. "When I told you that day in town I'd seen your boyfriend kill Lord Harry, there in the water meadow, and you'd best make it worth my while if you didn't want it known."

"Marie!" Mr. Murray moaned, his face broken by grief.

"It was my *brother,* Archie!" she said. When her husband just shook his head in disbelief, she turned to Robert. "You believe me, Robert. This was all my brother's idea."

"How did your brother know about the shipment of government money if you didn't tell him?" Murray asked.

"I let it slip accidentally," she said at once. "I had nothing to do with it except trying to protect my baby brother." It turned out eventually that her baby brother was one Henry Fanshawe, age thirty-five.

As the explanations were becoming complicated, Robert decided it was time to call in McAdam. He sent Lollie to Oakbay for our carriage. When it arrived, Robert and Lollie accompanied the Murrays to Chilton Abbas, where they were interrogated in the roundhouse. George had come in the carriage as well, to lend a hand.

"This may take a while," Robert said to me before leaving. "I'll return to Oakbay with Lollie when we're through in town. You'll be there?"

"Of course."

An intimate smile touched his lips and was echoed in his dark eyes. "Good. We have some unfinished business to discuss. Try if you can to get a few hours' rest, my dear." He had never used that endearment before or just that tender tone of voice.

"What about me?" Isaiah asked, when the Murrays were being trundled into the carriage.

"I'm taking you to Oakbay," George informed him.

"Would you mind having him there until I return?" Robert asked me.

"He'll get away!" I said, disliking such a responsibility.

"I'll speak to him," Robert said.

He took Isaiah aside for a private chat. I don't know what Robert said to him, but before leaving I heard Isaiah say, "I only dunnit 'cause she *promised* to take me to Lunnon." In any case, he went along quietly to Oakbay in the Murrays' donkey cart with George and me.

"I never bin in a carriage before," he said, smiling at such a rare treat. He looked so thin I could only feel sorry for him and hope that Robert could ease his punishment.

Robert was to stop at the Smoggs' cottage to inform them what was afoot. He left with the others. I was happy to see he had put his pistol away.

Dawn was breaking by the time we reached home. Rooks and swallows wheeled in a pink and indigo sky. Isaiah immediately asked for food and George took him to the kitchen.

I was filthy from head to toe from romping through the meadows and graveyard. There was no time for sleep, only to make a fresh toilette and meet Auntie in the breakfast parlor at the usual eight-thirty. I gave her an edited version of the events that had transpired. She took the notion that I had had the story secondhand from George. I didn't feel it necessary or wise to tell her I had been an active participant.

"I saw it coming, of course," she said, much to my surprise, as she had never mentioned any suspicion of the Murrays. She noticed my shock and continued, "I mentioned Mrs. Murray's fate line, did I not? I didn't like to tell her, but I knew something of this nature would occur. I gave it a few years, but perhaps she's closer to forty than thirty-five. That would account for the discrepancy. There is no arguing with the evidence of the hand."

No more was said of Robert's fire hand. I took my sketch pad out to the park as an excuse to watch for Robert's return. As I left, she said, "Have Isaiah sent up to me, Amy. It would be interesting to read that whelp's hand."

I feared she would hear an unedited version of the night's activities and went quickly out to the park as soon as I had notified Lentle of her request. The time I waited flew by in pleasant dreams of the future. It was going on eleven o'clock when I heard the carriage coming up the drive. I raced it to the front door and was there when it stopped.

Lollie got out first, looking exhausted but happy. "Well, it's done," he said.

"What happened?"

"We might as well go in and let Aunt Maude hear it as well. It will save repeating it." We all went up the stairs to the double oak doors.

Robert looked leery. "How has Isaiah been behaving?" he asked.

"Auntie was going to read his hand when I left. If he had made a run for it, I would have heard."

Auntie had heard them arrive and beat Lentle to the door to greet them. Isaiah was no longer with her.

"Did you ever hear of such a thing in your life!" was her greeting. "I mentioned to Amy that I had foreseen it all, of course. Let us have the details, Lollie."

The gentlemen were seated. I ordered coffee, as they looked as if they could use it. I didn't think they had had breakfast and asked Lentle to serve lunch as soon as possible.

Robert let Lollie tell the tale, interrupting from time to time to hasten it along or straighten out a point.

"It all started in London a month ago when Mrs. Murray found out about the shipment to the navy. She was in hock to her eyes because of her gambling. She got her brother to arrange the theft and bring the money down here to wait a few months until the talk had died down. She didn't want it kept in her own house, so Fanshawe hired a room in a nearby village. Meanwhile Lord Harry had got a line on Fanshawe—he's no stranger to the law courts—and followed him down here."

"Mrs. Murray never said much about that brother. Now we know why!" Auntie exclaimed. "We heard plenty about the solicitor from Norwich, but very little of the brother."

"Yes, well, he's nothing to boast of," Lollie said impatiently. "When Lord Harry began asking questions, Fanshawe wrote to his sister. She convinced Murray to come home for a spell, so she'd be on hand to manage affairs here."

"I thought it odd, her being home when the Season is on in London," Auntie said.

"Fanshawe used some other name, but Lord Harry had a good hunch who he really was. He was trying to find out who Fanshawe was working with—how he found out about the shipment— which is why he was asking us about Fanshawes, Amy. I daresay your telling him Mrs. Murray was a Fanshawe before marriage made him suspect her. Fanshawe admitted to Lord Harry that he knew where the blunt was, to lure him to a quiet spot to kill him. Isaiah had been snooping and had seen Marie and her brother together in the meadow. His only mistake was that he thought the brother was a boyfriend. Isaiah even saw the murder. Since he couldn't find Fanshawe, who had raced back to London, he accosted Marie to buy his silence. Marie insists she knew nothing about the murder, but it's pretty clear she engineered the theft at least. McAdam has sent a notice off to London to pick up Fanshawe. We'll hear his story in time."

"Who was it who bashed you in the meadow the day we found the money, Lollie?" I asked.

"It was Fanshawe, with a little help from Marie. He had taken a room in an inn between here and Woking, using a different name, and used to visit Marie when Murray wasn't about. They saw us in the meadow that day and hid behind the hut. They were there when I found the money and lay in wait till you left to bash me. When Maitland suddenly showed an interest in buying Chalmers's farm, Marie hoped to put suspicion on him."

"She was the first one who told me Maitland was buying the farm. She didn't mention he was taking a mortgage," I said.

"No more he is," Lollie said. "He's offered for Hadley's bran-faced daughter and been accepted. It's her dot that will buy the place, or make the down payment at least. Hadley is backing the deal." We ladies had a deal to say about this.

"Dash it, I've lost my place. Where was I?" Lollie said.

"At the shepherd's hut," Auntie reminded him.

"Right. From there they hid the blunt in those thorn bushes on Maitland's property, but they knew they couldn't leave it there. Marie knew Renshaw was an agent, so they couldn't hide it at Beauvert. Since they knew we were searching the meadow, they took the notion of hiding it in our cellar. It's fairly close by and wasn't likely to be suspected. Only they didn't know about the coal chute and broke the lock."

"I saw two people that night," I said. "So it wasn't Mr. Murray with Marie. It was Henry, alias the tall stranger. He did exist, Lollie."

"Yes, we thought it was Renshaw and his tiger," Lollie said. Robert lifted an eyebrow at me. Lollie continued, "Isaiah was becoming persistent in his demands, so Marie decided to take him into her confidence and use him to retrieve the money. She told him she'd take him to London and start him out as a foot-boy or some such thing. Well, she couldn't leave him behind, knowing so much. Then she had that party to throw us off the track and try to make things look normal."

"How deeply is Mr. Murray involved?" Auntie asked.

"He knew nothing about it until yesterday," Robert said. "Marie became worried when things got complicated, so she told her husband that Henry had stolen the money and hidden it in your cellar. Isaiah was to recover it and go to London with them. Murray agreed to help her on the condition that she return the money to the government. Anonymously, of course. They'd fly it to London at once, using the pretext of the election to account for their sudden departure.

"He had already decided not to run in the next election. He wanted to get Marie out of London, away from bad company. She agreed; whether she actually meant to give up the blunt is a moot point. I wager she thought she could bring him around her thumb."

I saw Auntie nodding and knew she was thinking about Marie's club thumbs and the fate line.

"Anyhow," Lollie continued, "Marie found out from her husband, who knew the details from McAdam, what was afoot at Oakbay last night."

"McAdam told us not to tell anyone!" I exclaimed.

"You may be sure Murray was pestering the life out of him. Murray wields a pretty big stick. McAdam told him everything he knew. It was Isaiah who suggested using the coal chute. It seems he's done it before. I expect we've been heating the Smoggs' cottage all these years if the truth were known. Marie gave Isaiah the bottle of drugged wine, with the label soaked off so it couldn't be identified, to give Leo Forten."

"Leo Forten would drink turpentine if it came in a wine bottle," Auntie said with a sniff.

"Once Forten was asleep, Isaiah slipped into the cellar," Lollie continued. "How the little devil ever hauled those heavy bags up the cellar stairs and out to the donkey cart by himself is a mystery. He must have made a few trips. It was agreed that Isaiah would hide the canvas bags in the empty grave and the Murrays would pick them up before dawn, run them back home and into their carriage, and take them to London to return to the government. Isaiah was to go to

London with them. Only we were there waiting for them," he said, and gave one of his smirking smiles.

"What will happen to them?" Auntie asked eagerly.

"Fanshawe will swing, certainly, for murdering Lord Harry," Lollie said. "I don't know how much weight Murray carries at Whitehall. He might manage to get his wife and himself off with a lightish sentence. The affair has opened his eyes to his wife's character in any case. She'll not hoodwink him again. Too bad for Murray."

"If you joust with a cat, you must expect to get scratched," Auntie averred, and continued on with a few other homilies. "It will provide a cold pudding to settle his great love of that trollop."

As it was getting on to lunchtime, Auntie suggested the gentlemen freshen up before eating. Robert was to remain for lunch. Auntie had a hundred questions to ask while we ate. Robert had two private meetings before he left Oakbay. One was with Auntie to ask her permission to propose to me. The other was with Isaiah. Both were successful, but I didn't learn about either until that evening. Immediately after lunch Robert and Lollie returned to Chilton Abbas to continue clearing up the details of the case.

Auntie and I were not far behind them. Beau's bull being loose on market day was nothing compared to the excitement going forth in Chilton Abbas that afternoon. Mrs. Davis was so agitated, she was running about the streets without a bonnet, and the drapery merchant closed his shop to allow himself and his wife to gossip without danger of someone walking off with a yard of ribbon without paying for it.

I was somewhat surprised to see Isaiah there. He was carrying a large parcel. Too large for him to have lifted from a shop shelf without paying. Probably a poached hare he was selling to the innkeeper.

"G'day, miss," he said. "You needn't report me to Monger. I'm on p'role. It's what they do in the army if you promise to be good. Colonel Renshaw set it up, seeing as how I'm a minor. I was more sinned agin than sinner," he said proudly. I assumed this was being misquoted from Robert, as I couldn't imagine Isaiah being familiar with the Bible.

I hoped Colonel Renshaw knew what he was about. If he had made himself responsible for that monkey of an Isaiah, he would have his hands full.

"I wonder why Renshaw bothered letting on he'd been in India," Auntie said. "There is no shame in having been one of Wellington's officers. Quite the contrary."

"Because of his dark skin. Where'd he get that, 'cept in Spain or India? Didn't want you to twig to it he was a spy, did he?" Isaiah replied, though she hadn't spoken to him. "Sojers back from Spain often switch to spyin'. Nabobs don't. As if the colonel'd bother with India."

On this condemnatory speech he continued on his way.

Chapter Eighteen

By eleven that night when Robert came, most of the details had been sorted out. Officials had been summoned by special messenger from London. Fanshawe had been arrested and charged with murder and robbery. He was less generous than Murray. He didn't hesitate to draw his sister into the mire with him. "What can you expect from a pig but a grunt?" was my aunt's comment on his behavior.

Marie was to stand trial for accessory to robbery and murder. She would certainly end up in Bridewell. Murray might have escaped with a fine in exchange for giving evidence, but he refused the offer. He would stand by his wife, but the feeling was that he might still escape without incarceration. His political career, of course, was over.

The Tories wasted no time. They had already approached Maitland regarding standing in the next election. Strangely, he refused. Auntie says that between taking on a wife and another monstrous farm, he'll have his dish full at home. Beau Sommers has been approached to be the new candidate. "Can you imagine Beau as an

M.P.? Lollie could do a better job," Auntie said. "Isaiah Smoggs could do as well." I doubt Beau even knows where Whitehall is, but the word is that he will run.

As soon as Auntie had satisfied her curiosity, she gave Robert a conspiratorial nod and said, "Can you come along upstairs with me, Lollie? I want you to move my dresser. I bump it every time I turn around."

"I'll call George," he said, unaware of her effort to leave Robert and myself alone.

"It will take both of you," she insisted, adding such grimaces and squints and nods that Lollie finally figured out something was afoot, though he still didn't know exactly what.

I heard him say, "What ails you, Aunt Maude? Is your liver acting up?" as they left.

"Alone at last," Robert said, and came to join me on the sofa by the cold grate. He seized my hand. "Now where were we this morning when we were so rudely interrupted?"

I assumed an air of artful confusion, for I was suddenly overcome by a fit of bashfulness as the fateful moment was upon me. "There was something you wanted to say, but you didn't think a graveyard the proper place," I said vaguely.

"So there was. Now what was it, I wonder?" he asked with a weighty frown.

"Robert! You were going to propose!"

"Ah, that was it! It slipped my mind."

"Oh, you beast!" I tried to wrench my hand away.

He grabbed my fingers and squeezed them. "Goose! You know what I want to say."

"Well, for goodness' sake, *say* it then." Impatience and nervousness lent a sharp edge to my words.

"Somehow this isn't exactly the mood I had hoped to establish. I envisaged a rose garden, moonlight, and romance—not a scowl and a push." I smiled at the folly of love, arguing at such a precious moment.

"That's better," he said softly, and drew my hand to his lips for a kiss. "Miss Talbot. I am very much in love with you. Will you do me the honor to be my wife?"

I was thrilled to death, but just a little disappointed at the stilted phrases. I just looked, and he continued. "Madly, passionately in love with you since the first moment I saw you sketching in the garden, with the tip of your tongue caught between your teeth and your gown spattered with paint. 'Now there is the very elegant creature to lend you a touch of class at Belview, Robert, my lad,' I said to myself. I shall love you forever and ever, till the oceans run dry. And if you dare to say no after leading me on scandalously for a whole week—"

"I didn't lead you on! For half the time I thought you were a thief!"

"But you were still interested. I can tell a hawk from a handsaw, miss!"

"I am neither a hawk nor a handsaw, sir."

"A little something of the hawk when you're

218

angry, my pet, but never mind. I'm feeling hawkish myself. I like a lady of spirit. How does a gentleman hawk propose to a lady hawk, I wonder? My wits are gone begging. We birds of prey don't ask. We take."

On that warning he snatched me into his arms for a most predatory and satisfactory embrace. The hawks were tamed to cooing doves before it was over.

At its conclusion he looked as dazed as I felt. He said in a husky voice that was trying to sound playful, "I consider myself quite compromised, Miss Talbot. If you don't want to find yourself saddled with a breach of promise suit, you will send the notices into the journals tomorrow at the latest. I shall have to be in London for a few days, which will allow you time to prepare your finest feathers for the nuptials."

"Will we be living in London or at your hops farm?"

"Oh, good, you said *we*. I take that as an acceptance. We shall be living in both places. I must spend some time at Belview. We'll be staying at the London house for the Season, of course, and from time to time when His Majesty has a little job for me to do. You won't mind?"

"I should adore London."

"There's just one little thing . . . " He gave me a look that was tinged with fear.

"You're not planning to go back to the Peninsula!"

"No, not that. It's Isaiah. I've asked him to, er, cmwthuz."

"I beg your pardon? I didn't understand—"

"I've asked him to come with us," he said in an unnaturally loud voice, and rushed on with his explanation. "I am responsible for his behavior, you see. In order to keep him out of jail, I undertook to make myself responsible for him."

He obviously expected me to rip up at this. I had already deduced something of the sort and approved. Being a rational lady, I also had a few reservations. "That should keep things lively," I said.

There was a racket at the doorway. Isaiah appeared in a clean white shirt that was several sizes too small, threadbare trousers the same, and bare feet. Both body and hair had been washed, however. I never realized he had such brilliant hair. It was as red and shiny as polished copper. For Isaiah, he looked extremely elegant.

"I had a baff," he announced proudly. His freckles stood out like beacons on the bridge of his nose. "Will this outfit do for Lunnon, Colonel?"

"That will do splendidly until we get you into livery," Robert replied.

"Liv'ry!" His eyes bulged from their sockets. "You mean a jacket with tails and silk stockings and all?"

"Yes, that is my meaning."

"Gor blimey. Will I get to . . . have to wear shoes as well?"

"The streets of London are hard. I'm afraid you'll have to wear shoes."

"Gor blimey!" he said again. Such a beatific smile alit on his freckled face that I hardly recognized him. I had never seen Isaiah actually smile before. I had often seen his impish grin, but there was more mischief than pleasure in it. This was a real smile of joy.

"Wait till I tell Ma that!"

"Why don't you tell her now?" Robert suggested. "I thought you were to spend this last night at home, Isaiah."

"I was afeared you'd snek off without me in the morning. I decided to sleep in your rig. Ma knows I'm here. She packed me up a bite to eat."

"I'll stop for you. That's a promise, Isaiah. Gentlemen don't lie, nor do they tolerate untruths in their staff."

"Me, lie?" he demanded. "Not to *you*, Colonel." One would think he was talking to God from the expression of reverence on his freckled little face. "What color's my liv'ry?" he asked, shattering the illusion of reverence.

"Dark blue, with gold trim."

"Gor blimey! I wish Ma could see it."

"She'll see it, when my wife and I come to visit Oakbay."

"You're marrying her then," he said, tossing his head to me.

"Miss Talbot has done me the honor of accepting my offer. It will be proper for you to address Miss Talbot as ma'am in future."

"Yessir, ma'am." In an excess of obedience, he saluted us both, then flew out of the room, his bare feet squeaking over the marbled hallway as he left.

"There's a deal of potential for either bad or good in the lad," Robert said. "It seemed a shame to leave him to sink into a life of crime for lack of guidance and opportunity. Besides, Chilton Abbas is too small for him. He's ready for London."

"Whether London is ready for him is another matter."

"If he gives you any trouble, any trouble at all, you have only to let me know."

"I'll do that, Robert," I said demurely. But having brought a colonel to heel, I didn't think I would need any help with Isaiah Smogg.

IF YOU HAVE ENJOYED READING THIS
LARGE PRINT BOOK AND YOU
WOULD LIKE MORE INFORMATION
ON HOW TO ORDER A WHEELER
LARGE PRINT BOOK, PLEASE WRITE
TO:

WHEELER PUBLISHING, INC.
P.O. BOX 531
ACCORD, MA 02018-0531